D0231688

BROOD

BROOD

JACKIE POLZIN

PICADOR

First published 2021 by Doubleday
a division of Penguin Random House LLC, New York.

First published in the UK 2021 by Picador
an imprint of Pan Macmillan
The Smithson, 6 Briset Street, London EC1M 5NR
EU representative: Macmillan Publishers Ireland Limited,
Mallard Lodge, Lansdowne Village, Dublin 4
Associated companies throughout the world
www.panmacmillan.com

ISBN 978-1-5290-5523-8

Copyright © Jacqueline Olson 2021

The right of Jackie Polzin to be identified as the
author of this work has been asserted by her in accordance
with the Copyright, Designs and Patents Act 1988.

All rights reserved. No part of this publication may be reproduced,
stored in a retrieval system, or transmitted, in any form, or by any means
(electronic, mechanical, photocopying, recording or otherwise)
without the prior written permission of the publisher.

Pan Macmillan does not have any control over, or any responsibility for,
any author or third-party websites referred to in or on this book.

1 3 5 7 9 8 6 4 2

A CIP catalogue record for this book is available from the British Library.

Printed and bound by CPI Group (UK) Ltd, Croydon, CR0 4YY

This book is sold subject to the condition that it shall not, by way of
trade or otherwise, be lent, hired out, or otherwise circulated without
the publisher's prior consent in any form of binding or cover other than
that in which it is published and without a similar condition including
this condition being imposed on the subsequent purchaser.

Visit www.picador.com to read more about all our books
and to buy them. You will also find features, author interviews and
news of any author events, and you can sign up for e-newsletters
so that you're always first to hear about our new releases.

For my mother

BROOD

I N OUR FIRST WEEK of owning chickens, four years ago, Helen stopped by to see the quaintness of the operation with her own eyes. I show the coop to any visitor who expresses interest in the chickens. Helen is an exception. She is my friend and thus shows an interest in my life. She does not otherwise care about the chickens.

Her visit took place in the brief interval before the grime of chickens had been established. The paint was fresh, the mice had not yet located the stockpile of various grains, and our garden had begun to sprout fairy greens and delicate purple stems of a plant whose identity I never confirmed.

Helen's questions were predictable, but my limited knowledge of chickens did not include the predictable questions or the answers to them.

"Do the chickens know their names?" she had asked. The chickens have never answered to a particular name but answer to any upbeat tone, names included, hoping for whatever treat may accompany the sound.

"Do the chickens like to be pet?" She took a step back

to indicate the question was not a request. "Are they upset when you take away their eggs?"

I didn't know the answers to any of these questions.

"Has a chicken ever laid an egg in your hand?" she asked.

"No," I said. And still, a chicken has never laid an egg in my hand.

I had not yet collected the eggs from early morning. Two brown eggs lay in a bowl of spun straw, one fair like milk tea, the other dark and a bit orange. At the time I did not know which chickens laid which eggs.

"Here." I placed the fair egg, which was also the smaller of the two, in Helen's palm. Her fingers did not soften to the shape.

"What should I do?" she asked.

"Cook it, eat it," I said.

"I mean now. What should I do now?" She did not hold the egg, but allowed the egg to rest on her flat hand, was only tolerating the egg for, I suppose, my benefit. The egg was not especially clean. The cleaner an egg looks, the more likely a visitor will accept the egg with grace and hold it in a manner befitting an egg, a force equal but opposite to the weight of the egg applied by a cupped hand, creating perfect balance and suspension in midair.

"Is it cooked?" she asked. "It's warm." She had seen me retrieve the egg from the straw, the straw worried down and out and up at the sides in the precise counter-shape of a nesting chicken, a bed of straw so primitive as to predate fire, and yet she wondered out loud.

"It's fresh," I said. "It's warm because it's fresh."

"Has an egg ever hatched in your hand?"

EVERYONE WONDERS if an egg, warm from a chicken, will hatch into a chick. The warmth of the egg prompts the retrieval of this otherwise remote idea. Among other triumphs of our generation, we have nearly extinguished the idea of an egg as a source of life. The confusion does not arise from the fact that people are no longer eating eggs or even that people are no longer cooking eggs. On the contrary, eggs are being eaten at a furious rate, and while the most adventurous preparations of eggs are crafted at the hands of professionals, in home kitchens the world over eggs are being prepared in more adventurous forms than ever before. The problem is not that eggs are bad for us or that eggs will make us fat. Rather, eggs are not as bad for us as we thought they were and eggs will not make us fatter than we already are. The problem is that people do not see the connection between an egg placed in their hand, fresh from a chicken, and the egg bought in the store. An egg that derives its warmth from existence inside the body of a chicken is far too fantastic to proceed as usual. If a fresh egg is placed straight into a carton versus an open palm, the confusion over what to do with an egg ceases to exist.

WEEKS AFTER Helen's first visit to the chickens, she returned with her boyfriend. He was a new boyfriend (and soon enough an ex-boyfriend) and she was trying to impress him. She had deemed her previous visit with the chickens sufficiently novel and called to warn me.

"I'm bringing Jack," she said. "Do you still have the half bottle of gin from last summer?"

"Of course," I said. "Percy doesn't drink gin and I'm trying to hate the same things as him." This last part was to make Helen laugh, but she only hummed, which meant she was snacking, most likely on one of the soft-baked cookies she's so fond of, which she buys in a paper sleeve and stores in the vegetable drawer behind a bag of carrots. The snacking, and therefore the humming, meant she was alone.

"Oh, good. Place it in the freezer, and could you do me a favor? Offer the gin early on."

Helen wanted and expected the whole experience to play out in the same fashion as her previous visit. She did not say it but I knew. Helen is a realtor, and realtors of all people should understand the disappointment of a second viewing. A realtor never makes a sale on a second look. If the first merits a second, the second requires a third. From surprise to disappointment to qualified relief. Helen's visit would be a disappointment.

I COULD NOT REPRODUCE or even approximate the experience. The chickens had stopped laying. The two brown eggs had been their last. If Helen had not called to suggest gin, I might have suggested it myself. The chickens would easily entertain from behind the curtain of midday gin. In the event I was wrong about the entertainment value of chickens or the power of gin, Percy suggested I give them eggs.

"There hasn't been an egg in two weeks."

Percy walked to the refrigerator and returned with a carton full of extra-large white eggs. "Give them these."

"No chicken of ours lays white eggs," I said. "And these eggs are cold."

"Helen won't notice and she wouldn't care. She'd prefer white," he said, which was likely true, though I would not give him the satisfaction of saying so. Percy took a small pot from beneath the stove, filled it with water, and set the pot to boil. I had forgotten to mention I was also morally opposed to his suggestion.

By the time Helen's leased BMW turned into the back

alley, three eggs sat steaming in a shadowed corner of the nest box.

"How do I grow a chicken from this egg?" Jack asked, the egg in his hand hot and gleaming. Helen admires confidence, falls often for the type, and I could see it was a flaw in Jack, preventing him from asking even such basic questions as "Why does the egg burn my hand?"

THE TIMER TICKS AWAY in the chicken shed. Each tick is bound to a counter-tick, like the one-two of a maraca, and behind that noise and counter-noise exists a faint buzzing of the electronics. The timer is programmed to turn on the heat lamp at 06:00, 12:00, 18:00, and 24:00. The coldest hour of the night is the last hour of complete darkness, but the lamp does not turn on at that hour. By six o'clock in the morning, the temperature has already begun to creep upward to its still frozen high. The chickens get by on thirty minutes of warm light every sixth hour because every moment of light increases the risk of fire in the coop. Helen has asked how we keep the chickens warm and I told her, "We have a heat lamp in the winter." I did not tell her the light shines for only one half hour every sixth hour and the first ten minutes of that warmth in the form of infrared light is absorbed by the frost caked on the hanging bulb. I do not want Helen to lose sleep over our chickens.

Do the chickens think of warmer times? They do not.

By the time a snowflake has landed, snowflakes are all a chicken has ever known. Theirs is a world of only snowflakes or only not.

At minus twenty degrees, the chickens refuse to leave the roost to eat the pellet blend I pour into the tin box feeder. The box hangs from chicken wire on two slim metal hooks extending up and back, attached to the sides of the metal box by a rivet that allows the hooks to swivel, but in the cold the hooks are frozen and the rivets are frozen and the box is frozen in an unnatural position, as if a spell has been suddenly cast upon it. In the spring I move the feed box to the outdoor run connected to the coop, but in the winter months, when a cold snap settles in, the chickens do not leave the coop for days on end.

Inside the coop, the temperature hovers between five and twenty degrees, but the water in the plastic jug exists as water, not ice, because of the small boost of heat provided by a sturdy jug-heating plate purchased for fifteen dollars at Farm and Fleet four years ago. Simple truths govern the care of chickens. Food and water must be clean and plentiful. Also, the chickens must not freeze to death, though it is unclear at what temperature this would occur.

G LORIA SITS IN THE NEST BOX, unmoving, as the other chickens busy themselves around her. For two days she has not strayed from the stagnant whorl of straw and dust and feathers tacked together here and there with bits of manure hardened into mortar. The last two mornings, she has made no motion toward the food or water as the other chickens gathered round in the usual melee, announcing themselves and jockeying for the choicest morsels. Unless she has eaten at night in the dark, she has not eaten. Chickens do not eat or drink at night because they cannot see well in the dark and the night is full of predators. The coop houses no predators, but the chickens do not know this. A chicken knows only what it can see. A chicken's life is full of magic. Lo and behold.

In the kitchen, the bottom drawer holds the most obscure utensils. Taking up a great volume of space inside the drawer is a device to core and peel apples: a three-pronged spire that holds the apple centered in a sharp-edged metal ring to extract the core, alongside a blade positioned at an angle to peel the skin from the curved surface. The machine functions exactly as intended, a perfect machine, if only a paring knife did not execute the same task with such grace and simplicity. The entire drawer is populated as such, by some false sense of necessity, though offhand I cannot think of a simpler tool than a turkey baster for watering a broody hen.

A chicken needs water, is like every other living thing in this respect, cannot live two days without it. In addition to a hen's need for water, the egg inside her needs water. Without water, an egg is just a piece of chalk.

Gloria's whole body bristles with the approach of the baster full of water. Her wings beat a dry knock against the walls of the nest box. She hisses the hoarse, pressed air of a snake and drinks one quivering drop.

BENEATH GLORIA IS AN EGG, large and cocoa brown. She does not lay eggs of this color. She lays eggs the color of a peach crayon and much smaller in size. Gloria has taken to sitting on all the eggs as if they were her own. Gloria sits with a crazy gleam in her eye, but that is just a chicken's eye. The eye of a chicken is all that's left of the dinosaurs, a little portal into the era of nut-size brains. Meaning cannot be derived from a chicken's eye because meaning does not exist there. But, also, the craziness of the eye obscures everything.

I shield my hand with a dustpan as I grope beneath her tail for the egg. She cracks at the aluminum with her beak. *Crack, crack,* despite no visible return. Who knows what she is feeling? A beak is not the same as a tooth, but I have several times chimed my tooth with a metal spoon and cannot imagine the aluminum, vibrating in my hand as it does, punctuated by sharp thwacks of her beak, is not sending an unpleasant message in the opposite direction, from beak to bone to bone, rattling the small cage that is a chicken.

Gloria triples in size when I reach in close, the way a pillow expands when you plump its sides. She executes the maneuver without thought. The movement of her feathers—the contraction of her skin and the corresponding bulk—precedes thought or takes the place of thought altogether. Gloria is wedded to the egg, not the idea of the egg. If the egg is removed, her memory of the egg goes with it.

The warmth of the egg is an original warmth and never fails to surprise me. Until we had chickens I never marveled at an egg, though I would expect it to have been the other way around: the incredible edible egg wooing me in the direction of chickens. Now that I have held this small warm place in the palm of my hand, I cannot help but wonder.

Gloria is curious about me. On an ordinary day, I don't dally. I pour the food, check for dead mice in the traps— the mice are too smart for this now, but I keep checking in the hopes of, I don't know what, a simple mouse—and make sure the jug of water isn't dry or tainted. But today I linger in the coop, tending to my tasks in the slowest possible manner. I miss the chickens now, even as they are still here.

I SHOULD HAVE SEEN this coming: missing the chickens. The same thing happened to our neighbor girl, Katherine, last year. She moved away and proceeded to miss the chickens in excess of caring about them in the first place, which is to say, she had taken them for granted.

Katherine was five then and still white-haired, and has always been a clumsy girl, prone to slow, premeditated movements. She had spent countless hours of her childhood lumbering after the chickens with her arms open wide. Chickens don't take lightly to broad wingspans. Whatever they saw in Katherine, they were right to flee her outstretched arms, held such for the very purpose of alighting on a chicken. I would have been so happy for them all, for the long-lasting diversion, if not for the chickens' abject terror.

Perhaps inevitably, Katherine's gait resembled a chicken's as much as possible. The running of the chickens was likely the only running she had ever seen, her mother being too big to run and her father too serious. Of course it isn't practical to move like a chicken. To move like a chicken benefits no one, least of all chickens, whose movement is a byproduct of breast-heavy breeding and can be neatly summed up as a failure to fly. Katherine must have been mercilessly teased by her classmates. The family up and left without warning six months ago, after school let out for summer.

NOT LONG BEFORE CHRISTMAS, a rumpled painting arrived in the mail. I would have thought Katherine had forgotten the chickens entirely—her enthusiasm had dwindled to almost nothing in the year prior to their move—were it not for the painting, the subject of which is a white chicken in a pink castle. On the back, in meticulous black marker, someone has transcribed the words "Princess Gam Gam." Here is a young girl who, in all her life, has known only two red chickens, a black chicken, and a gray chicken, yet she paints a picture of a grade-A white chicken in a princess castle. I hate to think of Katherine painting chickens so poorly so long after leaving, not to mention the failure of attention. The painting hangs in the coop, held fast to the wire by a clothespin, and the clotted tempera gathers dust.

THERE WAS A MAN with chickens in Riverton who woke one morning later than usual. My mother told me this story. She lives in Riverton and knows everything that happens there. Her voice sharpens as her stories progress so that I cannot think of this story without the ending ringing in my head.

There was a man with chickens in Riverton who woke one morning later than usual. The sun was high, though the world was frozen, and the chickens cried out in the usual cacophony that accompanies the arrival of a steaming egg into the world. Percy translates this noise as: "Guys, guys! Look what I found!" He does a passable impression of a surprised chicken and he does it often. People always laugh, because he looks like a fool and foolishness is a look people appreciate on others. Though I must admit, if I had not married Percy years before, his impression of a chicken having just laid an egg would not have swung me in that direction.

The hens clucked and crowed over their perfect parcels,

but the rooster was silent. That's strange, the man with chickens in Riverton thought. He looked outside and saw nothing out of the ordinary. On his way to the shed he spat once upon the ground to test the cold, whereupon it scattered on the snow like metal shavings. The chickens wore their feathers puffed into jackets and quibbled as usual, but the rooster was nowhere to be seen. Well, dang it all if the rooster hasn't gone off, the man thought. There had been a fox once, so the man looked around for signs of a fox: lost tail feather, trail of blood, tuft of orange fleece caught in the fence's coil. Nothing. Well, dang it all if the rooster hasn't gone off, the man thought; having thought it initially, he was now confirming the thought with all the existing facts. He went inside to scratch his head over the missing rooster. As he wondered, he looked out the window at the chicken shed. The weather vane was pointed in no particular direction, more down than out. Wait a good goldarn, I don't have a weather vane, he thought. He did not. He had a rooster, frozen solid on the roof of his shed. The rooster kept his post until the spring thaw, glued to the roof by a thin sheet of ice. When the ice melted, the rooster fell to the ground with a soft thud. I cannot remember why my mother told the story of the rooster, but the fact remains: you'll know when it's too cold for a chicken.

L AST WEEKEND I visited my mother in Riverton, two hours east of the city. I was born in Riverton and moved away after high school with no intent to return, yet it often seems, throughout my brief determined visits, that I have never left.

Percy had flown to Los Angeles for a three-day interview with a prestigious university. He had been driven to campus from the airport by the same person who, at a summit of ideas last fall, encouraged Percy to apply. In a matter of months, Percy has become so invested in the notion of teaching I've nearly forgotten it wasn't his dream all along, or even his idea. Percy has not taught a class since he was in graduate school. Rather, as his primary qualification, he cites a tenet of his work: the movement away from orthodoxy. Should Percy get the job, we will need to find the chickens a new home. It is my wish for my mother to inherit the chickens.

The chickens can fend for themselves several days on end, barring catastrophe. A scrap-wood box with greater capacity for feed hangs on the wall for these times when the tin feeder is not sufficient. The tray underlying the scrap-wood box is leftover decorative molding, which looks frivolous but is the opposite. The self-dispensing jug holds three quarts of water, enough for three days, and, in the absence of mice, the scrap-wood feeder holds food for a week. The mice are never absent, have been present in force from the moment four fifty-pound sacks of pellets and scratch were poured into a plastic storage bin in the garage, the shifting crush of grain a siren song to every mouse in the neighborhood. The famine was over.

There is no telling how much food the mice can stash in their hidey-holes in a week's time. Regardless of the measures we've taken to eradicate them once and for all, the mice are rampant, and songbirds fly in through openings no bigger than a walnut, and squirrels enter through the pophole on two legs, standing straight up in royal procession. As do the rabbits that linger in the lettuce, fat and slow, like zaftig garden trolls.

It is impossible to calculate our chickens' needs with so many mouths to feed and so much of the grain falling to the soiled ground, where it remains until scraped and folded and lifted away like the rolled dough of some medieval pastry. The mailman has suggested, not unkindly, that our chickens are overweight. He is an immigrant from a poor country and his notion of chickens is un-American.

But I am open to the idea that our chickens are overfed, given the amount of food scattered on the ground at all times.

MY MOTHER is perfectly suited to look after the chickens. She is raising two goats whose radius of destruction is far greater than that of chickens, and the mice are already well established, not just in the faded red shed and the garage and the careless treasure of my mother's lifelong heap of compost. The mice also have free rein in the basement and the inner walls of my mother's home. If the goats are not proof enough of her animal-loving spirit, the red shed with white trim is home to a flock of pigeons and a three-legged cat, all of whom she spoils. While I do not think my mother is prepared for the idiocy of chickens—pigeons being intelligent birds with coachable qualities—caring for the chickens will be just one more arc of food on the skyline as she tosses kibble in every conceivable direction.

I did not alert my mother to my visit, did not want her to fuss over me when I had come to ask a favor, and did not want to provoke the deep dish of odds and ends held together with a can of creamed soup. I called my mother as I filled the car with gas at the Kwik Trip in Riverton, where milk was on sale for ninety-nine cents a gallon. I surveyed the improbable savings papering the windows as the phone rang four times. The message on the machine has not changed in twenty-five years, despite the machine itself having been replaced on several occasions. I pictured my mother outside the red shed counting heads in the bitter cold. When I pulled into the driveway, that's where I found her, framed by the entrance of the small building, scratching the white chin of the black cat as the final act of her morning routine.

She scratched the cat as I parked the car near the house and walked down to meet her. Wind lapped my face with its shrill tongue. My mother's red hand against the white and black of the cat was startling to behold.

"Is everything okay?" she asked.

"I left a message on the machine," I said. "How cold is it?" I was not curious; I was complaining in the form of a question. My mother does not tolerate complaint in any form. She thrust her chin from the nest of her scarf, thus baring her neck to the cold.

MY MOTHER has upheld her solemn vow upon recent retirement to not buy anything she can make herself. For the average person, this does not include much: a vase of cut flowers or an elaborate salad. For my mother, a former home ec teacher possessing a great wealth of antiquated skills and an even greater measure of stubbornness, the list goes on and on. Like any of Percy's theoretic models—he cites my mother as proof of voluntary simplicity—it is a lovely lofty idea that shatters completely upon contact with the real world.

"Where's Percy?"

"In California. The finalists are being interviewed."

"Good for him. How many are there?"

"They didn't say."

"I always thought he should be a teacher." My mother says this of anyone she likes.

I poured myself a cup of coffee gone cold and placed it in the microwave.

"It's yesterday's coffee," she said.

"Percy does the same thing at home."

My mother smiled. "If there's one thing I don't understand, it's throwing out perfectly good coffee."

The coffee was not perfectly good. I rummaged through the refrigerator for cream under the watchful eye of my mother.

"It's much simpler to drink plain coffee."

She poured herself a cup. We sat down at the same time, which seemed to be her point: the economy of just plain coffee.

"I'll take you out for lunch. Someplace nice," I said.

"There's no place nice and I just had breakfast. The most I could eat right now is a donut."

"Fine, then. A donut. Where's the best donut in town?"

"You can't beat a homemade donut."

"Mom, please."

I PULLED INTO the Kwik Trip for the second time in an hour. There were two orange booths near the bathrooms. My mother requested a cream-filled donut and took a seat to ensure it would not be claimed by someone else. I would have thought no one sat at these tables in the faux-fruity breezes of the swinging bathroom doors were it not for much evidence to the contrary. Gouged into the plywood edge of the table were names I recognized.

None of the donuts were labeled. I chose the fattest donut from each of three racks as my mother looked on. The girl working the register wore a heavy jacket in protest of the cold. She was too young for me to know her, but I was sure I had seen her pinched face somewhere before.

Back at the orange booth, my mother had laid a cotton napkin on the table in front of her, along with a knife and fork from her kitchen drawer. This is something my grandmother used to do, carry silverware in her purse for just such occasions. How long before I carry a fork with me everywhere I go? Or a purse, for that matter? I don't think I am like my mother, or her mother either, most of all because I am not one. I am twenty years older than my mother was when she had me, twenty years estranged from the life she had. Sometimes I think of the unbroken line of women, all of them mothers, that ends finally with me—the whole of them wielding forks and purses and shaking their heads in disappointment.

"That's the oldest Thompson girl," my mother said, which meant I had gone to school with her mother. The girl behind the counter had the same pained expression, and the lids of her eyes were the same terrible shade of blue. The whole town is this way to me, familiar but worse. The drugstore is a pub now, and the dress shop is a thrift store, and the cinema shows one movie, three times a week. "She was a bad student but a nice girl," my mother said too loudly.

"We might need to find the chickens a new home."

"But you love the chickens."

"We can't take them with us."

"I thought nothing was decided."

"If it happens, is what I'm asking. Would you want the chickens if he gets the job?" I did not tell her the chickens had not laid well since autumn, had laid two eggs in the last nine days, and the week before that, nothing at all.

"I don't want to think about it unless it happens," she said, and she quartered a donut filled with cream.

As we walked to the car, the digital clock on the county bank confirmed what I suspected: it was colder than when I had arrived.

THE NEXT MORNING I woke full of worry in my childhood bed—the chickens' water had frozen overnight or the mice had staged an uprising or the heat lamp had finally burst into flames, igniting the layer of dust that clings with a certain tenacity to the lamp's protective shield because of the aspirated body oils of chickens collected there, a grease fire, a chicken-fat fire, and if a good Samaritan tried to extinguish the flames with water, the whole coop would explode.

I accompanied my mother on her morning circuit, our breath trailing behind us all the way to the house. I have never felt sure of the motions of caring for goats. I had thought caring for chickens would be a transferrable skill, would, at the very least, extend to the ilk of the hobby farm, but my experience with chickens has yielded no such skill. The more I care for them, the less I know.

"What's this?" my mother said. "The heater must have broken."

The water had frozen in the goats' heated tank. But the heater was not broken, was still chugging along, its rations of heat lost to the brittle cold. I thought of my frozen toes and then of the chickens. When a chicken's foot freezes, the skin turns white forever. If a chicken with frozen feet fell from its roost—and why wouldn't it?—the feet might break clean off. I shuddered and my mother scowled.

The goats rasped the ice with their tongues, leaving no mark. My mother pushed them aside and chipped with a shovel while I returned to the house to boil a pot of water. By the time I returned in a steaming cloud, the ice was already broken, and the pigeons fed, and the cat scratched, and the dust swept from the small room full of feed where my mother keeps a gallon drum of peppermint candies as treats for the goats.

THE COFFEE BELCHED to life in the old percolator. "I suppose whoever's watching the chickens will want them," my mother said.

"No one's watching the chickens."

"Helen wouldn't want them," my mother said, though she has met Helen on only one occasion. "And fresh eggs would be nice for breakfast."

I arrived home just shy of noon to find four chickens, all feet accounted for, and no fresh eggs.

P ERCY SAYS no news is good news. The interview was a success of the unquantifiable variety from which Percy needed to recover. Toward this end, he had donned a terry robe over his usual pajamas and placed a pillow on the low table so that his slippered feet might ride high in symbolic repose. His theories would go on proving and disproving themselves without him, hopefully in that order. In preparation for his trip, he had spent every moment of the last two weeks reacquainting himself with his own ideas, and was pleased to verify he had long championed a shift to the service sector. The prestigious university had all but confirmed its interest. He had heard nothing.

"I'm going to miss the chickens," Percy said. He prides himself in gleaning exactly one pinprick of insight from the camera obscura each time he travels.

I had no doubt Percy would miss the idea of himself as a man who owns chickens, a man whose life is thus simplified and complicated simultaneously by association with them. Raising chickens is high on Percy's list of paradigm shifts, but would he miss the chickens? It seemed the chickens, having already fostered Percy's dear idea of himself, would prove incidental. I would miss the chickens, was already missing the chickens, which I regarded as the true test of one's capacity to miss anything: the visceral anticipation of doing so.

The township of the university does not allow chickens. If we brought chickens to the township, we would violate a civic code. This is just the sort of lawless act of community Percy considers panacea, even if, to the neighbors, the chickens are just a morning racket and a pervading odor in spring. But I cannot bear the thought of the chickens being taken from us there, taken to some distant farm, and then what? Only my mother would care for the chickens and ask so little in return.

O N THE COLDEST NIGHTS of the year, I plug a space heater into the orange extension cord in the chicken shed and make sure all the doors are closed. This includes forcing a too-big piece of insulation board into the chicken-size pophole that serves as a doorway to the caged-in outdoor portion of the coop. The space heater can otherwise be found wherever Percy used it last, most often by the low table in the living room where he props his feet. The living room is loosely considered Percy's home office or, for tax purposes, considered Percy's home office in the strictest sense. Percy is not the type of person who embraces slight discomfort as a means of productivity. He is the other type: he who lounges to facilitate understanding.

Percy's desk takes up the southeast corner of the room, obscured by houseplants, three of them clippings off the fourth. The plant thrives on negligence, and so they thrive. Somewhere beneath a philodendron lies a notebook bearing jargon.

. . .

STRANGE THINGS HAPPEN at forty degrees below zero. Sound travels without impediment, skin freezes faster than the perception of cold, wet things become rigid corpses of their former selves. As for water, forget water. Water gives up completely. Aspirations, forget those, too. Subzero temperatures are a renaissance of the original aspiration: to survive. Chickens are poorly equipped for survival, but because a chicken has no memory of what came before and no thought of what comes after, winter is no psychic shock. Last year there were fifteen consecutive days when the temperature did not rise above zero and dipped several nights to forty below. The only comfort provided by such morbid temperatures is the promise of being perfectly preserved.

A chicken's perception of cold does not likely resemble ours in any way, is instead the sensation of skin stretching and lifting as the feathers rise. In response to cold, every contour feather composing the outer shell of a chicken shifts upward on its slender shaft. Thousands of feathers reach up and out in one synchronized movement. A chicken does not think to do this, does not decide. A chicken's body simply does, divorced from the knowledge of cold and its possibilities. Beneath the contour feathers, the downy underfeathers also rise, filling the space beneath and trapping the air warmed by a chicken's life. The down of a chicken functions only to make and keep space between a chicken and the outside world. When the world outside is below zero, that space, or some fraction of it, and its bit of fluff are the margin for life.

Throughout last year's cold spell the heater remained in the coop, just outside the wire divide. The chickens huddled together on their perch, as close as their puffy coats allowed. Miss Hennepin County, the alpha, marked the shortest distance to the source of heat, flanked on either side by Darkness and Gloria, while Gam Gam marked the farthest remove. Gam Gam is the lowest in the pecking order, because she would be the first to die either way. The social arrangement of chickens represents their statistical advantage. The pecking order is a natural order, bullying as natural selection. Perhaps this is why the pecking order has always unnerved me.

J OHNSON WANTS to see you," Helen said. "Can I bring him over?" I have never known Johnson to express a clear desire—he is only a year old and slow to speak—but I hoped he wanted to see me. I cannot help that I care very much to be the kind of person children want to see. Helen went on to say that the woman who watches Johnson had come down with strep and, though Helen herself wanted to see me, could she leave Johnson with me while she met a client to drop off keys? Her words bounced as she hit a pothole, which meant she was on her way. Through the southeast window I saw the rump of Helen's BMW round the corner toward our drive. It didn't matter why they had come, I was glad to see them.

"He'll sleep the whole time," Helen said. "He hasn't slept all day."

She set the car seat on the kitchen counter, then reached up and back to correct her posture. Helen is built like a tulip, tall and stoop-shouldered, but not without grace. It is too soon to tell if Johnson resembles her in any way beyond his wide gray eyes. I hovered over him to comfort myself with his smell. Helen was already late to deliver keys to the new owner of an expensive property I had cleaned the week before; the property's value is directly related to its distance from our neighborhood.

It is difficult to sell a home in winter. I know this because I clean every house Helen sells. I try not to think of how many houses Helen would need to sell in order for her husband to quit his job. He works in oil fields all over the world and is almost never home. Before Helen became pregnant with Johnson, she claimed the secret to a lasting marriage is a husband who lives elsewhere. I've always known Helen to make light of her difficulties, but a family is different from a marriage, in many ways that would probably not occur to me, save for the most obvious, that a family is binding by nature.

"I'll be back soon," Helen said, and closed the door behind her. Of course Johnson woke then and began to cry.

His cheeks flushed from pink to red. I stripped off his jacket, only to find another jacket, hooded, and fastened with buttons, and beneath that a sleeper, also hooded, and zipped from the leg up. Under all of this security, his rage had been stoked into great rashy blotches. The tepid bottle left by Helen made him want to throw something and proved convenient, and the throwing required screaming, and in this way he arrived at a full-fledged tantrum. His forehead felt hot and a bit spongy where a vein had come to life, pulsing up and over the curve of his scalp into his fine hair. He kicked in my arms until I placed him on the rug, from where his screams took on a whole new dimension. I picked him right back up, and it did not seem fair that, though setting him down had made things worse, picking him up did not make them better. Johnson's face was borderline purple. Percy was in the next room but guessed correctly that he had exhausted his right to remain there. He stepped into the doorway with a wary smile.

"Does he feel hot to you?" I asked. Percy placed his hand on Johnson's forehead then on his own.

"He feels hot."

I know this much about children: everything serious begins this way.

Percy could not find a thermometer, if only so he could leave to buy one. Meanwhile, I rocked Johnson gently, then less so, then held him in every possible way: over my shoulder, against my chest, on my lap with knees bouncing, which seemed to calm him. His crying leveled to the most basic "WHAAA, WHAAA, WHAAA" as if straight from the pages of a comic book. It would not have surprised me if his frantic little punches had been accompanied by a "POW, POW, POW." Finally I pinned his arms to his body and tucked him between my elbow and the curve of my waist. This is one way that chickens like to be held.

His cries tapered to a trembling whimper. Twice his own pathetic bleats reminded him to cry all over again, but I held him fast. With a last tremendous wail and shudder, he fell asleep on my hip with his head in my hand. His cheek filled my palm like a giant apricot.

By the time Percy returned from the store with a thermometer, two bottles of medicine, and a stuffed elephant as big as a Saint Bernard, Johnson's forehead bore the imprint of a button on my shirt.

HELEN CAME BACK in high spirits and assured me that Johnson was fine, he had been too tired was all, and crying that way always makes him hot, and there is nothing to do when it happens but let him cry himself to sleep.

Only a mother knows. This is the cardinal rule of motherhood and the great source of a mother's power. It stands to reason that if you are not a mother, you know nothing about it.

YEARS AGO, as Percy and I drove to a farm south of Burnsville to buy chickens, we agreed we wanted at least one chicken with fun-colored eggs. Throughout the drive we debated the merits of blue versus green. When we arrived at the farm, the matron was carrying a bucket of water to the outdoor run, and she finished the task before greeting us in the driveway. She was brusque and serious and, because I had never seen jeans as dirty as the ones she wore, I got the feeling she needed every dollar we had promised her—we had come for four chickens. To ask for eggs of a special color seemed suddenly too frivolous to voice out loud.

"That one seems healthy," I said, pointing to the chicken we named Gam Gam. I knew nothing of a chicken's health or the signs, but her red feathers turned purple near the tail, with the overall effect of a rainbow.

Once three chickens had been chosen by the splendor of their plumage, Percy asked, "How do you tell the color of a chicken's eggs?"

"Look at their ears," the matron said. "A chicken with white ears lays white eggs and so on." Then, having judged us accordingly, she added, "This one here lays real small eggs. I call 'em 'half-cal.' Some people prefer those."

Back in the car and a mile down the country road, Percy said, "I didn't know chickens have ears." I had been thinking the same thing. It frightened me that we shared such a thought, and frightened me more so that we shared the same instinct upon having it: to hide our ignorance from the chicken farmer. I suppose I had thought she would find us unfit, or that Percy himself would. Farmers are wise from experience, so it follows that we knew nothing. There was no better time to be reminded of this than at the beginning.

I WOKE EARLY with Percy asleep beside me but did not leave the bed until late, instead staring at the ceiling and listening to the sharp pops of the house as it shifted in the cold. The chickens were not yet awake, I knew from the eerie silence. And when they did rise in chorus, sometime later, I could tell Percy fed them by the abrupt end to their noise. I rarely do this, leave the feeding to Percy, and cannot remember a time when I lay in bed until just before noon. I think there is something wrong with people who lie in bed this way, unmoving, perhaps even pretending to sleep, as I pretended during Percy's whole morning routine.

I HAD NOT SET FOOT in the Oaks for six years. Back then I did not call it by any name; I knew it only by the number of its address and the tall trees lining the walkway, so close on either side the roots seemed poised to lift the concrete from its path. At the time I cleaned ten houses a week, a routine I quit in part so I might never return to that house again. But now I clean only for Helen, governed by no contract other than our friendship.

Helen gives a name to every house she sells. She says the story of the Oaks is one of hierarchy. Stairs occur randomly in sets of three throughout the house, each room existing on a slightly different plane. I cannot imagine the benefits of such design because I work with a vacuum. Hierarchy is not a perfect plan; rather, it occurs most often as an absence of plan—i.e., the natural order of things. Take the basic unit of social structure, the family. No family exists without hierarchy. Even Picasso, who famously never spoke the word "no" to his children, and whose methods Helen champions as her own, was still the father of his house. It was his choice to withhold the word and no amount of provocation could persuade him otherwise. When Picasso told his children to play and be free, it was both his deepest wish for them and an order.

I MADE MY WAY straight to the farthest bathroom, not because of what happened there, but because I always start with the bathroom. A bathroom must be cleaned with complete detachment. While detachment in general is useful for cleaning, a bathroom requires the steely reserve of a doctor. Each droplet, splash, and fleck must be approached

with equanimity, each hair with the opposite of curiosity, each wad of sodden paper with blind efficiency. Once
my disregard for the bathroom has been achieved, I am
unstoppable—a force of complete objective action. I sweep
and scrub undaunted. I perform bold acts of elimination
without pause. I polish and shine with a frenzy indistinguishable from rapture, buoyed by the thrust of sheer
doing.

The bathroom was just as I remembered: the toilet with
its wooden seat and lid, the thick-walled tub flush with the
floor, the floor itself pieced together in six-sided tile—an
exact replica of the wire composing the chickens' fence. I
was four months pregnant then and had spent the morning
cursing the curry I had eaten the night before. I should not
have eaten it or should not have gone to bed right after or
should not have spent the morning on my hands and knees
scrubbing in a cloud of bitter lemon cleaner as the pain
crested over and over. It is strange now to think that for
some time, as the pain persisted and worsened and finally
clutched my insides into a bone-white fist, I blamed the
curry. I was, I suppose, armored by the thought, and to
have thought otherwise, to have thought rightly all morning long, would have made no difference.

I had hoped to outweigh the risks of pregnancy at my
age with sheer desire. I had waited so long—our whole late
marriage had been preoccupied with this. All would be

well because I wanted it completely. As I doubled over on the clean bathroom floor, the truth was revealed as pure physical fact. The blood was warm and red. The pain was lasting. I don't know how long I lay there, every part of me clenching or waiting to clench. When I stood I could not make sense of what had come out of me. I could not separate what was me from the tiny piece of her.

L IFE IS THE ONGOING EFFORT to live. Some people make it look easy. Chickens do not. Chickens die suddenly and without explanation. Before sunrise, the thermometer outside the kitchen window read fifteen below zero. I had woken with a jolt, could not remember closing the pophole door the night before, whereas I could distinctly remember leaving the pophole open for as long as possible to freshen the coop before locking it up. But the act of locking, the cold metal of the bolt between my fingers—unbearably cold, dangerously cold, because the bolt is too slim to grasp with a fatly mittened hand—I could not recall, nor flipping the switch on the dusty heater. If I had not done one, it followed that I had not done the other, these actions belonging to the same set. Coat, hat, scarf, boots. Mittens last of all because the closure of each boot is nothing more than two long strands of soft leather, to be bandaged around the canvas upper of the boot and tied in a droopy bow.

The snow crunched like dry cereal beneath my feet. Frost covered the window of the coop, so thick I could not see the chickens on their roost. But the plank door of the pophole was secure and inside the heater steamed, webbed in dust. The water in the self-dispensing jug had begun to freeze. Ice grew in clean shards from the edge of the red trough. With the hook of my finger I plucked the lip of ice from the water, where it fell to the floor and shattered into pieces with the merry tinkle of a glass bell.

The chickens blinked to life on their perch, four in a tidy row, poufed to the max, chirping softly like chicks—so are the days of chickens, each morning a bright and solitary gem. I was swept up in an irresistible urge to hug them all, such was my relief; had half expected—more than half, but not quite fully—to find them in a firm heap, Miss Hennepin County crowning the pyre, the last to fall and still the closest to the flame.

BACK AT THE HOUSE, the lace of my boot had come undone. The boots are a simple construction, a bit too simple, in fact, but that does not stop people like me from buying these boots like our grandmothers bought toasters, fully believing the boots will change our lives. There is a secret to the spare design of these boots that few people know. I learned the secret at the library, where a man in the lobby eyed my boots hungrily, his shoes the kind of historic shipwreck you find one of on a beach somewhere. His backpack was no doubt host to a collection of similar objects, not to mention the frying pan tied with rope to his belt of the same, and his hat, which was first and foremost a pillow of the standard size. He cited the make and model of my boots to boost his credibility. "The people at the North Pole wear ten pairs of inserts in those boots. Without inserts, you'll lose your toes," he said. This was perhaps one subject of his expertise. He switched his attention to a girl beside me with faded pink hair: "If you rub lard in the roots and don't shower, the color will last longer." He left us, all the wiser, to join a tattered woman holding a baby no bigger than two chapped hands. I could only hope his arcane knowledge would be of use to her.

A dogsledder in Ely, four hours to our north, makes these poorly lined boots, has made a lucrative business of it. The insufficient lining is most likely a problem that has never occurred to him, being of hardier stock than most of the world and also future generations.

AT SUNDOWN on the coldest nights I return to the coop to throw four handfuls of corn to the floor, one palm of grain for each chicken, though it stands to reason via rank and file that Miss Hennepin County gets a good deal more and

Gam Gam a good deal less. Once eaten, the corn burns hot like a furnace, warming the chickens from the inside out as they roost through the night.

I approached the door of the coop with no trace of the morning's alarm, though the frost was still thick on the window, had melted only in the warmest hour of the day then frozen again in a burst of stars. The chickens greeted me with a chorus of garbled noise. I pried the four-cornered lid from the bucket of corn. Oh, the corn makes them happy! The garble gave way to the singular *tuck tuck tuck* of pleasure at each and every kernel. Gam Gam lay in the corner, could not be lured with the clatter and scatter of corn. My nearness did not provoke her, nor my shadow as it fell on top of her. I reached in toward her, then it seemed I reached right through her, beyond her flat feathers, until I touched the very meat of her. She was cold. Firm and cold.

THE NEIGHBORS WATCHED ME carry the clear plastic bag containing Gam Gam's body from the coop to the house— I had placed her in clear plastic so that her presence in the freezer would not be mistaken for something else. They did not notice the bag contained the lifeless form of our youngest, dearest chicken, though we spoke over the low-lying fence regarding the next winter storm and the shoveling it might require.

Percy and I took Gam Gam, frozen and frosted in sheer plastic, to the veterinary clinic at the university. By the time we traversed the many bleached hallways to the diagnostic unit, her body was soft and wet. We paid five hundred dollars to be shocked by the youth of the doctor, who told us the tests revealed nothing at all. It is a small, albeit costly, comfort to learn our ignorance is on par with the ignorance all around us.

"She was my favorite chicken," Percy said.

"I don't have a favorite," I said, but it had been Gam Gam.

CLEANING has no magic formula. The secret is to go at it long enough to get results. The results of cleaning can be observed. Reflective surfaces, when clean, multiply the light in a room, filling a room with light. Smooth glass, polished metal, old-fashioned wood cared for in an old-fashioned manner—all become a source of light. Light bounces from clean surface to clean surface, making light of all in the room. An unclean house accumulates dust and therefore darkness.

In a clean house, flat surfaces continue uninterrupted. The eye does not stop to investigate a crumb or a clod of dirt fallen from the bottom of a shoe with deep tread. Vision travels the length of a clean surface to the point where the surface ends. The eye lands on an object of its own choosing rather than the errant scrap or heaped towel.

A heaped towel in low light—or any discarded garment reduced to compact stillness on the floor, but especially a towel, given the heft and pile—resembles a dead animal. In an instant, the mind corrects the eye: there lies a towel because here is a bathroom full of towels. The mind corrects with such speed that the dead animal exists in memory as a single frame of a moving picture, no less retrievable than any other frame, though the odds of retrieval are less than with the many frames of towels, and attached by the thinnest thread to misconception.

ON THE FIRST FRIDAY of February, late in the afternoon, I recovered the neighborhood quarterly from the front step beneath an inch of fresh snow. Headline: "Crude Oil Blast Radius Includes Much of Camden Neighborhood, What Might This Mean for Us?" The article that followed consisted only of the same words in a much smaller typesetting. There is a lesson to be learned from this. No one knows what our existence in the crude oil blast radius might mean for us but, printed as such, in tremendous font, it can't be good. The crude oil passes by us on its way from North Dakota to the refineries. The train barks at all hours, heavier than before. Because of the heft, the reverberations of the rails travel in waves through the ground and reach the house through its foundation, shaking the walls imperceptibly, though if I place a hand on the wall, I feel it, like the buzz of bass, as the train passes. The walls hum and the wood trembles and the plaster crumbles with the force of the train, the smallest outward force compared with the train's thrust forward.

The vibrations have caused a rift in the cement floor of the basement, and along the rift, a series of small holes from which a trail of ants—tiny ants, as if just born, or perhaps a miniature variety of older, wiser ant, and they do seem wise, always collaborating in the most peaceful manner—has marked the start of spring for the last three years and a giant spider emerged last summer, having feasted on them, reaching out one fibrous leg, poised to devour or retreat. On the afternoon I spied the solitary leg of the spider, the light shone through the blocks of soda fountain glass lying flush with the ground above and caused a projection of the leg on the basement floor opposite, an even larger fibrous leg.

One morning, weeks later, another giant spider, perhaps bigger, perhaps not—it is impossible to tell the actual size of a spider, a spider being more of an idea than a thing, though it is also a thing, a living thing, whose size depends entirely on its posture and whose life depends on no more than a wayward glance—sat on a washcloth in the kitchen sink. I felt I could not proceed in either direction until the spider was unrecognizable as such.

I cannot recall how I killed the spider, but there it was, clenched in a twiggy fist. The mop was almost certainly involved as it was within arm's reach. Percy arrived shortly after, hurried by the noise. To aid in my recovery, Percy assured me the spider in the sink was the same spider from the hole in the basement. I had never considered that the life span of the previous spider might extend beyond the two weeks since I had seen it last. Percy's reassurance had the opposite effect. Days later, a spider of the same ilk ventured out from behind the freezer in the basement as I retrieved a loaf of bread. Percy took care of it, he assured me, which made two giant spiders of the same variety in less than a month—muscular brown ones, perhaps of the necrotic rot family—assuming I'd seen all the spiders and assuming Percy was right about two being one. If he was wrong, there were three, and one was unaccounted for.

THE SUGAR MAPLE in the backyard is dying. I am trying not to think of it this way, but each season brings with it new evidence. The couple who owned the house before us carved their names in a heart shape too deeply into its trunk. The bark within withered and died, leaving a scar in an approximate heart across one-third of the tree's girth, which could not have been good for their marriage. The tree is tall with an elegant shape, bowing toward the house in a long gray arc, the smaller branches reaching upward in clean lines. If I were to wrap my arms around the trunk, my fingers would not touch on the far side. To lose the tree would be a blow to the whole neighborhood, to say nothing of the thirty feet in one direction, most likely our kitchen and the dining room beyond.

Each year the tree suffers new grievous loss: three prominent branches downed in a windstorm last April, a cryptic message scrawled by woodpecker months later in a sprawling rift that appeared as if by lightning, and, in the fall, a new fissure in the bark at the base of the tree, some distance removed from the barren heart and, I believe, unrelated, that wept a viscous trail of sap into the ground below, preserving the sparse grass there in its amber crust. I don't know what determines the will of a tree, but for our maple, a heart-shaped abscess slowly expanding outward is reason enough to die. The tree has given up. There is no other explanation for the constant litter of its limbs on the ground below and the green mold on its exterior and the unspectacular color of last autumn. When the cold ebbs away or perhaps winter ends overnight as it sometimes does, the tree will be one season closer to firewood.

As much as I am able, I keep the chickens far from dying. But the simple fact remains that chickens have delicate constitutions. The chickens don't care about my gestures toward life in a traditional sense, but most of the time they don't die, which is the most primitive form of gratitude. It does not follow that chickens die as a form of ingratitude. No one knows why chickens die. The only thing to do for a sick chicken is to check if an egg is stuck in her egg chute—"egg chute" being the informal term, Percy's, because he prides himself on his informality. A chicken with an egg in the pipe walks more like a duck than a chicken. Of course, if you've only ever seen the walk of one or the other, or none at all, this information is of no use.

Gam Gam became egg bound once, in the year before her death. "Egg bound" is the technical term. Gam Gam had been our most agile chicken before the obstruction. Could outrun the others with ease, which proved fortunate because the other chickens had singled her out as the low-

est in the order, often surrounding her in the back corner
of the coop and picking the fresh feathers emerging on her
tail until all that remained was the wilted flesh of her bare
bottom, speckled with blood. The first and only sign of the
egg bound inside her was a great wag in her posterior, her
sparsely feathered butt low and pendulous, as if she danced
to irresistible music. She watched me with a worried look.
It did not occur to me she walked like a duck, though something was clearly wrong. Still, for all the trouble it caused
her, she was not opposed to moving. On the contrary, she
seemed spurred to movement.

Percy had been in the living room digitizing the contents
of his milk crates and effectively switched tasks without
moving an inch, was now researching chickens and their
demise, without even a hesitation of his hand's methodical
swipe. He announced we should place Gam Gam's butt in a
bucket of warm water, or we could prod her egg hole with
a clean finger.

"How warm?" I said.

"Let me see, simmer for two hours, hmm. Not too warm,
I guess."

I WAS FEELING quite protective of Gam Gam. She did not
run from me, nor did she resist as I scooped her to my
chest; either she had developed a sudden affection for me or

she was dying. Her pulse beat a frantic little tune. I prodded her rear and felt a firm mass there. For all I had prodded a chicken, it might have been the basic underpinnings.

"She's sick," I said.

"It's more like existential constipation," Percy said, then watched for my reaction to his smart remark.

Gam Gam's toes curled into my favorite gray sweater, hooking the loose knit. It was easy to mistake the mechanism for trust, stuck together as we were, like a Scandinavian system for hanging things. I carried her, tight against me, to the bottom of the stairs. From there I was unable to proceed, had never given the stairs much thought, until now, the stakes raised to the nth degree with the bird, light as porcelain, panting against me. Four simple stairs of average width and height. But I could not see where to set my foot; Gam Gam lay directly in my field of view. I had climbed these stairs ten thousand times and never wondered where to step or imagined the particulars of getting it wrong. The bird would fare no better than a bag of pretzels.

"Could you help me?" I stuck my elbow toward Percy. "I can't see where I'm going."

He took my arm with both hands and led me straight up the stairs. "Here's the first," he said, "and then two more, and the last, and voila," he declared, though he did not soon let go of my arm.

Gam Gam's stiff feet clutched my chest and could not be undone. Rigor mortis, I thought, which spurred me to action. I tore off the sweater with the chicken inside and placed the whole in the sink full of suds—the soap Percy's own helpless touch. I held Gam Gam afloat in the frothy water and felt her soften. Whether or not chickens can swim, and I don't think they can, she began to paddle, the tread of her toes like dirty cutlery beneath the ripple of my sweater.

I did not see the egg emerge but I can attest to its silence. I had placed Gam Gam in a cardboard box, big enough for a chicken or, to be exact, twelve bottles of wine, and turned my back to consider what might make the most convincing nest: spring greens gone sour in a Fresh-Tite bag or a pound of dry spaghetti. Meanwhile, the egg left Gam Gam's body and landed without a sound on the cardboard, looking for all the trouble like an ordinary egg. I had expected the pop and spill of champagne.

C LEAN IS NOT a natural state. Of all the circumstances that may randomly occur, cleanliness is not one of them. Cleanliness is a temporary state, inseparable from the act of cleaning. This is never more clear than in the privacy of one's home. A single non-cleaning person will face this truth eventually.

Dirt is the most natural thing in the world but often undesirable. To keep dirt at bay, we enshroud ourselves against it, board by board. The placement of a wall is arbitrary—nature does not begin here and end there—but not without meaning. A wall suggests that resources are available on one side that are not available on the other, which, in this sense, is the opposite of sharing.

The neighborhood is all boarded up. It is safe to assume what lies behind the locked doors and boarded windows is not worth any trouble, but the boards remain. Perhaps to deprive the teenagers their musical joy of breaking glass. At the corner shop, which is always changing hands but never changing, a hole the size of the end of a Q-tip appeared overnight in the plate-glass door. Around the small hole the thick glass forms a perfectly concentric crater. Any number of things could have caused the hole, but I can think of only one.

Our neighborhood has failed to reach its potential. It is not a good neighborhood and perhaps it never was, but it was supposed to be. A failure to reach potential is the problem of our time. Just look around at the sunk cost of human life everywhere. As an example, I can, at this very moment, see out our front window a man in a red jacket, hood held aloft by the bitter wind, sitting on the bench by the parkway, watching the house kitty-corner, waiting for the shade to be cocked halfway or a series of on-off switches of the light or whatever sign indicates the arrival of new drugs in a predetermined place. Twice I have seen a fast-food bag tossed from a fine-rimmed vehicle, shortly thereafter retrieved by a man seated on the bench, once this very man in the red jacket, perhaps both times if he is in possession of more than one winter coat. The man retrieved the bag and threw it in the nearest receptacle, but not before peeling a game piece from its exterior and extracting a small package from the inside. The men of our neighborhood are not otherwise in the habit of sitting on benches or disposing of trash.

Despite eager talk of potential, the value of our house has sunk for years, unpredictably, until sinking became the most likely outcome. Since then the value has continued to sink. At a certain point, we will be better off tying our phones to a stick with a napkin and heading west.

PERCY BOUGHT the house before we met. The woman he dated at the time thought the house was charming and she was right. It is a charming house. She knew nothing about real estate, nor did it matter to her. She is long gone and the house remains and the location is unchanged. I love this house for its stalwart good looks and its determination to be worth something here or, rather, our determination that it be worth as much here as anywhere. Toward this end, we painted each room—some of them twice, having not nailed the color the first time around—planted a fruit tree, and hung two strings of white lights, though the bulbs have proven too fragile. We purchased a bird feeder, then a squirrel-proof bird feeder, broken now due to its own powerful mechanism. The feeder sensed the presence of squirrels and sent them, cheeks full of seed, catapulting into space according to the laws of centrifugal force, feeding the squirrels and entertaining them at the same time.

It is a good time to leave. The trains pass by at all hours of the day and night. The spiders have emerged. The death of the sugar maple looms large on the horizon. Whoever lives in the house kitty-corner is selling drugs, and pious Rita next door to us and directly across from them suffers from dementia and paranoia. I once carried a misplaced newspaper to her front door, where I was greeted by the lens of a large telescope.

I know only three things about real estate: location, location, location. This is enough to grasp our situation.

TRAINS USED TO RUN two times a day in a charming fashion. Three-quarters of a mile down the road, the engine would cough to life, followed by the heave-all clang of each car bumping up against the car in front of it, signaling the beginning of the show. During these intervals of nostalgic rumbling, I would often look out the kitchen window, over the alley and the back-door neighbors' giant carrots, watching the colorful paint jobs on the passing cars for a marvelous rendition of a vulgar word.

Now the trains pass by at all hours. The noise of the train is irregular, sometimes jarring on account of the weight of crude oil, sometimes gentle, when the cars are filled with lightweight goods: tennis shoes or modern electronics, fresh off the boat from the vast international marketplace, or bags of popcorn from Mankato headed overseas. Even popped corn must travel great distances so that we can live life unencumbered by popping it elsewhere, free from the motes of grease that float in the air, finding each other and becoming drops of grease on our walls and in our lives and, of course, inside of us. We will never make popcorn again, having bought it for a price that seems cheaper than fair. We will tell stories of popping corn, and the children of the next generation will enact whatever obscene gesture is the future of rolling one's eyes. Sometimes when I lie awake in the night, the sound of the train is a human sound, shrill and rising. When this happens I know I am on the edge of sleep. Oh, the baby is crying, I think, and still I fade away.

OUR FORMER NEIGHBORS called Tuesday evening just after dinner and well before bed. They must have called from their landline in Iowa, because both Cal and Lynn were on the phone. The timing was off throughout. If the conversation had been with only one person, I would have known the reason for calling was being circled rather than said, such were the silences. I also was not talking, which was how the silence came to be complete. The call to my phone had caught me quite off guard. Percy had been friendly with Cal and I had been less so with Lynn. Why did they not call Percy? Or rather, why did Cal not call Percy, who sat on the couch deducing the conversation from the lack thereof? (Percy enjoys nothing more than the awkward theater of real life.) Why did Cal and Lynn call at all, the two of them together like an old-fashioned way to spend a Sunday afternoon? I wasn't aware they had my number and was spending my small part of the silence thinking of the many ways others are more skilled than myself at acquiring personal information.

"Do you suppose— Oh, Cal, not now— But I thought— How's Percy?" they said.

"He's right here if you'd like to talk to him."

Percy picked up his notebook, was now working.

"We don't want to interrupt."

The silence persisted and, in doing so, deepened, was almost unbearable or had become unbearable already, and the proof was yet to appear. It is the current fashion to experience all aspects of life to the point of breaking. In this sense our silence was very fashionable. I'm not cut out for the luxuries of self-deprivation, could never sustain it, especially if the luxury consists of doing nothing at all. "Don't be strangers," I said. "Stop by and visit the chickens when you come to town," which turned out to be a good example of unbearable silence yielding something even worse.

"Saturday," Cal said. "We'll be there Saturday."

"If the offer still stands," Lynn said.

Of course it would be fine, good, it would be good, and the chickens would love to see their lovely daughter ("lovely daughter" my exact words, having blanked on her name, though "lovely" wasn't the exact word I was searching for—"Katherine," I remembered a moment too late), and it didn't matter to us if we were even home, they could just visit the chickens and stay as long as they liked. I hoped we were not home.

I would have to make a welcoming treat, which was not much trouble but would weigh on my mind to an extent that made up for it.

In the cupboard, all in a row like an encyclopedic set, we have twelve boxes of mix for brownies. The great wealth of brownies-to-be is what remains of Percy's recent exposé. He had heard somewhere that the two eggs required by every box of brownies had originally existed in powdered form in the mix itself. At some point, because the mix proved too effortless, robbing homemakers of all agency, the powdered eggs were removed so that fresh eggs could be added by hand, thus empowering the women who buy cake in a box. In Percy's proposed experiment he would bake two batches of brownies every day for a month: one with powdered eggs, one with fresh. (I can only assume the abundance of brownies was a previously established fantasy.) He announced the end of the experiment abruptly, halfway in, as addendum to the fact that he had gained ten pounds and having determined the experiment did not, in any notable way, debunk his original theory: fresh eggs do not get better results, are in fact less reliable, introducing a greater margin for human error. Hence a well-received essay in a little-known journal claiming we would rather contribute poorly than do nothing. So the boxes remain.

I will have to clean the coop before Lynn's visit. On several occasions, Lynn has shared with me her respect for my cleanliness. "I do not clean well," she said, "I think in too small of categories." In the years Lynn lived across the alley drive, I had never been inside her house to confirm the state of it or the numerous categories therein.

I once watched Lynn clean her car throughout a long afternoon. I noted her progress at intervals through the kitchen window, her broad butt in cotton twill raised to the sky. The task seemed to repeat itself over and over with no visible results, save for Lynn's permed hair blown every which way by the force of her cleaning. Each stage of the process involved an elaborate bottle for administering cleaning agent, or a mutation of the vacuum, or, later on, a powerful spigot affixed to the garden hose, until the car, finally, at sundown, looked the same as before.

M OST PEOPLE do not think of chicken skin beyond whether it is a part of the chicken they prefer to eat. Some like a sandwich consisting of little else and others remove the skin in any form, no matter the preparation, placing it ceremoniously on the edge of the plate, where it acts as a fleshy magnet to whatever lies close at hand. The skin of a living chicken acts in the opposite fashion: flakes, falls away, disperses.

Chicken dander floats in the air for hours at a time before settling to the ground. If, during the dander's slow descent, a chicken flaps its wings or a gust of wind enters the coop or a visitor coughs or gestures emphatically, the dander will be flushed back up into the air, prolonging its fall. Despite the limited effect of gravity on the fine particulate of the coop, dust accumulates faster within the coop than elsewhere. Everything that enters the coop becomes dust over time. While this is true of all things everywhere, the stuff of the coop becomes dust so quickly: the food upon pouring, when scratched, and soon after as dung; the straw when strewn or trodden; the chickens themselves as skin and feather and scale. Chickens bathe in dirt to rid themselves of hazardous particles, whether or not the particles exist. Chickens' lives are governed by doing, not knowing; therefore it must be done, this routine maintenance of ruffling dirt hither and yon. To all of this puff and chaff, add the particulate of whatever animals are drawn to the excess of the chickens. And then, as the cherry, twice a year Percy holds each chicken by its feet upside down—a chicken held this way stretches its wings—and douses the chicken with organic powder. The sprinkling takes place outside the coop, but the powder, a talcum so fine it squeaks underfoot, clings to a chicken's feathers for days, muting the shine, before finally slipping free and, sometime later, coming to rest on the ground below. Onto the floor of the coop falls the caustic powder, smelling of oranges, along with whatever once lived on the flesh and feathers of the chicken, though it stands to reason the powder does not discriminate between that which is welcome and that which is not.

If not for Lynn's visit and her reverence for my cleaning, I would not clean the coop. I do not clean the coop in winter. I jump to the task with gusto each spring, but, until then, the dust piles up, making plush the interior. Plush green bin full of straw, plush heat lamp (flammable), plush utensil for gouging dandelions, plush garden gloves patched with duct tape and unused since the first week in November, when the need to rake was blotted out by an early and lasting snow. When contact is made with any plush object a shower of dust falls from it and reveals the lesser object beneath. If the bag of oyster shell with its quilted surface is removed from the top shelf, or the bag of grass seed with its quilted surface from the same, the shower of dust makes a squalid snow globe of everything below.

ON THE SECOND OF NOVEMBER last year, the snow began in a noncommittal fashion. The flakes dropped into the sky on a cold wind from the north, causing the flakes to circle without landing, all the while accumulating in the air. For hours the snow dropped and swirled, never reaching the ground, in a thick blur of white on a backdrop of white with the grass still green beneath it. From out the kitchen window, the world looked like a painting just begun. When the wind died abruptly, in the midst of the crawl of rush-hour traffic, the snow landed all at once on the cars inching away from work in the city. Percy was driving on the interstate at the time. His bumper hit the bumper of the car in front of him at the same moment the bumper of the car behind him hit the bumper of his car and so forth and so behind. Everywhere, people stepped from their cars to check bumpers, only to find they had driven into the snow separating one car from the next. The cars had pinned the sudden fall of snow between them.

When the snow began, the chickens paused their scratching amid the tattered hostas. Chickens do not like the cold, but snow has nothing to do with cold inside the narrow corridor of a chicken's mind. The snowflakes moved in every way like a plague of houseflies; the strange, swift storm was a chicken's wildest dream come true, though it is likely chickens do not dream, stuck as they are in the present moment. At that moment, the sky was full of the busy flotsam chickens are specifically designed to intercept. The chickens busied themselves plucking flakes from the air one by one, over and over. If I did not know better, I would say the scene looked playful, but chickens are not playful creatures. Chickens eat, drink, and sleep and do little else. On rare occasions such as this the outcome is indistinguishable from play.

I DID NOT USE my CleanMax Zoom for cleaning the coop. I care too much for it. I retrieved the shop vac from the basement and hobbled up the steps with my arms around its girth, the perilous hose trailing. I propped the screen door open by sliding a metal washer alongside the hydraulic mechanism to halt the closing of the door. Propped open this way, the glass frosted over with the breath of cold.

The chickens panic over the shop vac each time I clean. If I could communicate such a complex idea, I would tell the chickens not to worry.

The chickens flew poorly into the wall—fly so poorly it breaks my heart—while I, thick hose in mittened hand, pawed at the pophole door with the other. The door was frozen in place, called for a solid kick with my soft boot. Toes ringing, the door flew open with a sharp crack, and the chickens scampered out in pecking order to alert the neighborhood of a small black hole in their living room sucking the surface from everything. The sharp cries of their bold pronouncement crowed over the alien shushing of the vacuum. I've watched terrifying movies whose soundtracks consist only of screaming over white noise, the terror born of the noise itself. But here, in the coop on this ordinary day, I was not afraid.

The chickens' world has threatened to end in the exact same fashion countless times before, but a chicken does not remember. A chicken lives each moment once and only once. The sky is falling and the busy squirrels do not care; the sky is falling and the plain sparrows do not care; the sky is falling and the hungry dogs do not care, save for Coco across the alley behind a wall of cedar fence, whose daily communiqué is an indecipherable brutal threat.

WE WERE HOME on Saturday because we had no plan to leave, and to make a plan would be to plan an escape. If I lived alone, that's exactly what I would have done, but Percy was home, is nearly always home, and I would not want him to watch me do it.

"Why don't you bake the brownies, so you can relax," Percy said. I had been thinking out loud about the brownies as I paced the room, was thinking of the brownies at that very moment and the small gap of time in which brownies are done without appearing to be. The brownies were not yet baked so that their warmth, straight from the oven, might mask their average quality. Cal would have to maneuver the extraordinary length of his wood-paneled wagon inch by inch into the driveway. I had watched him park the wagon so many times I could summon the whole scene, his head ratcheting front to back over his right shoulder like a man hunted, the brake lights on and off and on again, then finally off. I might conceivably crack two eggs and mix the brownies in the interval provided, if I prepped the pan. "I will bake the brownies at the last minute," I thought aloud. From where I stood by the living room window, there was not a car to be seen on the parkway.

The snow outside was a grimy white. A dust of new powder blew over the surface like a trick of the eye. A man and a woman and a girl threw a red ball back and forth. The winter has been so long already and as cold as always, I could not imagine the fun of it. The ball itself had collapsed with cold. The limp plastic caught a shaft of wind, flew a good ways out, and the girl lumbered after it. *Fee fi fo fum.* It could only be Katherine.

"Lynn? Katherine? Come in," I called out.

"No hurry," Cal said. "We're just playing ball." Lynn's large hands were tucked snug in the armpits of her quilted coat, beneath the straps of an adult backpack, and Katherine wore no gloves at all.

"Boots off," Lynn said, as they entered the house.

Katherine shed her boots without stopping and bounded to the kitchen, where a window over the counter faces the coop. She stood on her tiptoes to scout the chickens. Katherine is not yet tall, but to see her this way—every inch straining upward—it is clear she will be. She will be tall, like her mother.

"I see them!" Katherine said. The hanging red bulb that

warms the coop had burned a hole in the frost on the window like a chichi portrait. The chickens sat beneath the heat in a tidy row. "Can we go?" She jumped up and down, rattling the pans in the drawer under the oven.

"Hold those horses, Katy," Cal said, "what do you say we have a seat and catch up with the neighbors?" He sat down beside Percy.

"Katherine, do you like brownies?" I asked. Katherine nodded, a bit hyperactively for so early in the day. Lynn shook her head no. I went to the cupboard, and behold. There on the top shelf, the bookish row of brownies had been replaced with a pink box tied with string. Oh, how Percy beamed from his signature divot on the couch. I shimmied the string toward the edge of the box. The tight fit gave me time to consider that the box might very well contain a pair of silken undies, the too-big box suggesting luxury. The idea of the undies was helped along by the shimmying motion of the string, the way a perfectly tight fit cannot easily be undone. The box seemed too big but less so when I considered the improperness of a pair of silken undies placed in the smallest possible box. How cheap it would seem to deprive them the luxury of space. I paused with the lid in hand, did not want to be the one to introduce Katherine to the concept of silken undies.

The box was full of pastries. Katherine fondled each one in turn.

"I shouldn't," Lynn said. "There's a potluck after the funeral."

"I'm sorry," I said. "I didn't know."

"A second cousin, is all," said Cal. Lynn bowed her head, then opened the small pouch of her backpack and took out a piece of gum.

"Would Katherine like to see the chickens?" I said.

All that remained of Katherine was half a frosted donut.

On went the long gray coat that covers my knees and the mukluks with their tedious laces. On went the soft scarf with tangled fringe and the bright orange hat, its brightness serving no other purpose than to prevent accidental shootings, which, in our neighborhood, is not completely beside the point. And, finally, the serious mittens lined in fur. I heard Katherine chirping just outside the door, but when I emerged, wrapped in my trappings like a roll of carpet, she was nowhere to be seen, her nonsensical chirps disembodied by the trickster cold. I saw the glow of her blond hair through the coop's frosted window.

"Do you think she remembers me?" Katherine asked. She offered her fingers to Gloria through the wide wire mesh. The chickens remember nothing, of course, not their chicken companions, not me, and certainly not Katherine, who seemed a full foot taller than when she lived next door.

Wind blew into the coop in sharp blades. The chickens would not venture outside without a bribe. When I returned from the kitchen, banana in hand, Katherine held Gloria in a tight embrace. Gloria gacked and fluttered, then fell under the spell of Katherine's gaze, perhaps noting the chicken in miniature trapped in Katherine's eyeball, or the eye's resemblance to a succulent grape.

"Can I keep her?"

"You can feed her this." I placed the banana in Katherine's palm.

"Will she eat my hand?"

"She's never eaten a hand." She has tried, of course, and failed.

"Ow, ow, ow, ow, ow, ow, ow." Katherine did not otherwise seem to mind it. "When she sheds her feet, can I have one?"

"Chickens don't shed their feet," I said. But I had never thought about the growth of a chicken's foot, even as I had marveled at the intricate piecework of its shifting scales, cut from the same cloth as the skin of a snake. Gloria's feet appeared larger now than ever before.

Katherine hugged the chicken to her chest. "Do you think she'll miss me?"

"She'll live," I said, though I could not be sure.

From where Cal and Lynn watched through the kitchen window, their old house could be seen off to the right. The new neighbors have painted the trim a buttercup yellow, which makes the siding appear dingier than ever, and the house has never looked worse.

"Off we go, little lass," Cal said, as he hurried her to the wagon.

"Can I say goodbye to the chickens?"

"You were just there," Lynn said.

"I didn't know we were leaving."

"Yes, you did, we have the funeral."

I watched the wagon bob into the alley and disappear.

SOME TIME LATER there was a knock on the door. Lynn stood in the doorway, her hand on Katherine's shoulder.

"Katherine has something she'd like to tell you."

"Gloria gave this to me." Katherine held a pale brown egg swaddled in Kleenex.

"Katherine," Lynn said.

"I'm sorry," Katherine said, and placed the egg in my hand, soft on my skin like a new bar of soap.

THE MOVE is not for certain. Percy is waiting to hear from the prestigious university, has heard nothing since his interview at the end of January. Despite his lack of experience, he is hopeful, on account of his mastery of jargon and his slow and steady track record of publications that pass through many hands. His last book became a popular object to be seen with, though there is no way of knowing the exact point at which people stop reading his work and continue to be seen with it. As much as possible I do not read his work, but I can attest to the fatigue of doing so. His books are difficult and therefore boring, and on top of this, Percy has always been curious about such particular things. I am never bored by his work because of my urge to protect him, piqued at every turn. But I imagine I am not alone in my relief that his theories celebrate modest output. Though the search committee has yet to disclose its decision, Percy maintains that the silence is meaningful, could mean, among other things, he is the last of the finalists. Still, it is a rarely acknowledged truth that he who gets nothing waits the longest.

"THE STRANGEST THING happened last night," Percy said. I doubted it. We had slept side by side. The odds of the strangest thing happening without affecting me in any way seemed slim. He said he had woken in the night to find a woman sitting on his chest. "It wasn't me," I said, and he said he knew that. He could see it wasn't me or, rather, could see me beside him, fast asleep, and yet he could not see her, this invisible woman, but he knew she was a woman, she had the aura of a woman, and he knew also it was no accident she sat upon him; if she had preferred to sit upon me, she could have, or if she had preferred to sit on no one at all, there was ample space at the foot of the bed between us, if in fact she was proportioned like a normal woman, and he was certain she was, though he cited no proof. What did he know? What did Percy know of the qualities and proportions of the supernatural woman? Unless, of course, he had touched her. Most men would, I should think, upon waking to a silent invisible woman presented on their person in the blear of sleep. I did not ask how he knew incontrovertibly it was a woman of normal proportion; I could not bring myself to ask. She sat upon him for what seemed a minute, though on this point he was less certain.

I know the aura he referred to, the aura of a woman, if that's what we're calling it. Our baby had been a girl. I knew this based on aura alone—i.e., for no reason at all. No reason but a certain quality surrounding her, which is to say, a certain quality inside me. In my heart I knew, prior to any test that might confirm it, and no test did. The time for testing became some other terrible time.

"I'm sorry," Percy said, "I wasn't thinking. I should have thought."

"It's nothing," I said. "Ghost stories always cause my eyes to water." Percy knows this about me, knows every one of my foibles, just as I know his: he is one inch taller than his license claims, and when he delivers bad news he holds the back of his head with one hand, as if expecting a blow from behind.

E VERY PREGNANT WOMAN wants a girl. If a pregnant woman thinks she wants a boy, she has not completed the thought wherein a boy is not a girl. When a pregnant woman learns she is having a boy she convinces herself the simultaneous feeling of disappointment has nothing to do with the particular outcome. Why wouldn't the halving of all possible outcomes yield disappointment? One moment anything is possible, a child could be a boy or a girl, and, inherent in this, any kind of either. Upon knowing which half of the possibilities remain, half of the possibilities have disappeared. The child will be a boy or a girl. When a pregnant woman learns she is having a boy, she convinces herself it will be okay.

Upon receiving the news that she was having a boy, Helen called to tell me, to be comforted by me. I sensed she had been crying even though, throughout our friendship of many years, I have seen her cry on only one occasion. It had happened many weeks before the phone call at a small cafe where we often met for lunch. Helen announced her pregnancy in the most matter-of-fact way. She had confirmed the test that very morning. It seemed she could not help herself, could not keep her secret a minute longer, but of course she had to tell me this way, the moment she sat down. In our friendship, this was her way of being. The news was a complete surprise to me and, upon seeing her excitement, the same old sadness returned. I could see Helen wanted me to be happy for her as she waited for my response. But for quite some time I said nothing and watched her eager smile slip away. She didn't wipe her eyes or make a sound or otherwise draw attention to the fact that she was crying. The tears just appeared on her face like any other feature.

When I answered the phone, months later, Helen's silence had the same breathy charge.

"Helen?" I said. I knew what she had called to say—it was a boy. Deep down I felt relief. Helen would not have it all.

"It's a boy."

"Hurray," I said. I could think of nothing else.

"None of the things I had imagined doing with the baby are things a boy does."

"A baby doesn't care," I assured her.

"My future has become a blank space. I can't imagine it."

All the mothers I know, save for one, have decided to have another baby. Some mothers come to this conclusion time after time after time. My friend with one child had only one child so she would feel less bad about consuming more throughout her lifetime. Her haircut is severe and requires much maintenance, and I am not sure she feels less bad about it. Helen will have to have another baby—a baby girl.

If our baby had gone on living, I, too, would want another. I suppose it would feel no different from the way things are.

THE CHICKENS have run out of food. The bulk of the feed is kept in a giant plastic box the exact length of a roll of wrapping paper and so large that, filled with anything other than the metallic garland and patterned paper it was designed for, the box cannot be lifted. I fill the box with pellets and scratch grains and have no intention of ever lifting it. The most I have ever managed to move the giant bin full of feed is one inch in the direction of the wall via a swift kick toward the bottom, resulting in a pop in my ankle and a sharp stab of pain. The box sits flush with one wall of the garage. On top of the box, there is a piece of cardboard I have fashioned into a funnel using staples and painter's tape. It is a contraption of passable function and the utmost scrappiness. Percy regards the funnel with a kind of reverence.

From the bulk container of chicken food in the garage, I fill three jugs that are otherwise kept in the coop itself. I have taken considerable care to remove all traces of soap from the jugs—formerly bottles of laundry detergent and the faded labels attest to this—before filling them, via funnel, with pellets and scratch grains. When a bottle of detergent nears the end, I fill the jug partway with water and shake. I use the diluted mixture in the same measure as its full-strength counterpart, thus extending the life of the detergent by a considerable margin. I have never noticed a change in the cleanliness of our clothes when using this watered-down detergent. It seems our clean clothes must be, at all other times, too clean.

AT THE FARM AND FLEET off Highway 62, I am in the monthly habit of buying two fifty-pound bags of layer pellets and two fifty-pound bags of scratch grains. I had made every previous trip on a weekend. On weekends, the floor help at Farm and Fleet is made up entirely of high school boys. The boys offer to load the bags for me, which they do without hesitation or strain. My request for equal parts pellets and scratch has never given them pause. On this day, because it is a weekday and the strapping youth are in school, an old man in the company orange shirt offered to lift the bags for me.

"I need two bags of pellets and two bags of scratch," I told him. The ease with which the words rolled off my tongue was a comfort in the strange land of halters and fleece. Before we had chickens, I could never have imagined walking into a store containing everything you need to be a farmer (plus a large supply of gumdrops and salted nuts) to request pellets and scratch grains.

"What's it for, chickens?" the man asked.

Of course it's for chickens, I thought. I knew nothing beyond what the package told me. There were chickens printed on the tight plastic weave of the bag where there might also have been sparrows and mice and an upstanding squirrel.

"Rich diet for a chicken," the man said. "Those scratch grains are like Twinkies."

"It's not all for one chicken. We have three."

"You want ten parts pellets to one part scratch. Any more and your chickens won't even bother with what's good for 'em."

He was right, of course. Our chickens ate only the Twinkie portion of their diet. The wholesome pellets were scattered everywhere in the coop and, if the pellets could be placed back in the original bags, would probably fill the bags to the top or more so—had most likely taken on moisture and now existed in greater volume than before. I asked the man to please load as many bags of pellets as would fit. The bags did not fit in the cart—he had piled them high—and when stacked in the car, the back hatch did not close completely. On the drive home, one bag occupied the passenger seat, secured by seat belt to silence the technology of the car.

I WATCHED FOR A CHANGE in the chickens' aspect or demeanor—glossier feathers, softer feet, the sudden realization they could fly—but the chickens looked the same and acted the same, and I could still have filled the pellet bags to the top with the pellets that had fallen to the floor.

While there is no way of knowing the cause of Gam Gam's death, the Twinkies cannot be overlooked, nor can I see beyond them. From all the well-meaning advice on what to feed a chicken, how had I arrived at a habit of 50 percent cream cakes? I'd made a practice based on bad information and could not even remember where the idea came from. It seemed there was nothing to stop me from making the same mistake again.

Oh, Gam Gam, I didn't know. I never feel smaller than when I am filled with doubt, such a small, small feeling, it's a marvel it can fill anything at all. Filled with doubt I shrink until I can hardly move, can do nothing but wait and see what happens.

T HE HOUSE ON THE LAKE is full of windows, so that
with each wipe of the glass, the floor seemed less
clean. My notion of progress was thus turned upside
down. I have always found it unsettling to place my
faith in process, wherein the promise of results is substitute for proof of them. But sure enough, the house
became clean, and as it did, the windows resumed their
function, blurring the boundary between inside and out.
When my work was finally done and the gleam of light
in the main room traveled every which way, the sense
of cleanliness was so encompassing—extended even to
the lake outside in its blinding blanket of snow—as to be
almost pure. I had the urge, not often arising as I work,
to share the feeling, though in all likelihood the feeling
could not be shared, because my own hand had set into
motion this dazzling brightness, and whatever I felt was
not separate from my role in it. Most work is this way,

I imagine, privately rewarding, and therefore cannot be shared. My first job cleaning was in college and, while it appealed to me for other reasons, my lasting impression of the job was this solitude. And so I have often come back to it.

I N THE LAST WEEK of March there has been only a flurry of new snow, and the old snow dwindles, carved into hill and dale by the winter wind, low spots melting into clear pools at midday, only to freeze flat in the night. Each afternoon is a quiet chorus—steady drip of a single drop, puddling; trickle in the gutter, soft but ecstatic—the slow swell of water, finally moving, having spent all of winter in one place.

Spring arrives earlier each year, marked most reliably by the return of the robins. Before having chickens I never noted the arrival of birds in the springtime, but now, because the readiness of worms concerns me, I watch the sky for the first dash of orange. It seems every year there are more of them, more robins this year than ever before. Of course, this is the way of the world—the more robins you look for, the more robins you see. They hop in the brown grasses and over the last knobs of dirt and snow, plucking whatever lives in the ground from it, and, afterward, sit in the barren trees and sing merrily. A bird's life is full of song and adventure, whereas a chicken has neither. Perhaps this is why I don't often think of chickens as birds at all.

JUST WHEN I THINK I have come to know the chickens as much as possible, they surprise me. Today, while the others slept, Miss Hennepin County fought sleep. I have never seen a chicken fight sleep, have always considered fighting sleep a form of ambition, so that now I must amend my view of chickens to include ambition in some raw form. I had watched the others fall asleep to her left and to her right, red combs in a row, the crepe of their lids shuttered down, each body buoyed by its own even flux. In the midst of the tidal calm around her, Miss Hennepin County would not allow it. Her eyes began to close, then sprung open in a movement so sudden it carried her head with the force. The snap revived her but not for long, and again her eyes began to close, and so on, over and over. The poor chicken. If only I could promise her safety.

I N THE BACKYARD where the chickens roam there are no robins. The worms have been reduced to such dire numbers there or the robins' absence is a primitive form of deference provoked by the chickens' regal carriage—head back, breasts forward, comb high on the head like a trophy.

Darkness is the great huntress. She is neither the fastest nor the wisest nor the earliest to rise, but she sees farther. Worms move below the surface or peek their wormy heads from the soil like slick antennas from the underworld. This morning I watched as Darkness ran from inside the coop through the pophole, out the gate of the chicken run to the cobbled landing at the base of the steps, to a sliver of ground between two stones, in order to pull from the earth a night crawler the width of my finger, which she stretched to the point of breaking like a rubber band until the creature hung from her beak, whole and limp. Inch by inch, the worm disappeared.

I was saddened by the worm, not because the worm had been swallowed in an ungainly and traumatic fashion, half ground to mash in the rocky entrails of a chicken while the other half dangled in midair—or I suppose in part because of this, the way it resembled torture of the highest order—but more than this I was sad to be sad about the worm when most often I am not. I give the average worm no thought at all, though on occasion I encounter a worm stranded on pavement and have saved such worms when the spirit moves me. Here one moment, gone the next. Poor worm.

A certain quality of chance encounter has always affected me this way, exposing the state of things to be desperate and inescapable: spotted egg on pavement amid its own slight spill, shrine at a road sign, blue memory snapping like the tail of a stuck kite.

YESTERDAY, as I walked a stretch of the parkway near our house, I watched as a sock fell from the shorts of a man walking ahead of me. He is an Asian man who looks quite old, owing, in part, to his hunchbacked posture. The man lives in a blue house—electric blue—with trim painted the same, lending the windows an eerie nakedness. Each summer I have seen him gardening there in a cone-shaped hat. The garden is plotted with sticks crossed high enough to walk stoop-shouldered beneath them and inhabited all year by a ragged scarecrow with an old broomstick for a spine. In the early spring, the man unfurls great sheets of plastic over the scaffolding of sticks in order to begin his garden while snow is still on the ground.

The shorts came as a surprise on a cold morning in April. From a distance, the man seemed a bit reckless on account of them, and therefore youthful, so that I did not, at first, recognize him. I have encountered this man for years on the parkway, often between his house and mine; he walks a greater distance than I, farther in both directions, and slower, increasing the odds that when I walk, our paths will cross. When I pass he nods in acknowledgment, though his head remains bent to the ground. His gait is such that he does not pick up his feet completely, causing undue wear to the bottoms of his shoes. The shoes are reinforced across the bottom and on all sides with silver tape.

As he walked several feet ahead of me, the sock fell from his shorts with incredible slowness. The friction of his movements—his feet shuffling, his shorts shifting, the wind against his body—caused the sock to fall in the slowest motion, as if a powerful time-magnifying device existed between the falling sock and my perception. The sock had no doubt spent the winter folded into this pair of shorts, stuck fast by whatever force holds two things together. The old man did not register the sensation of the sock in any way as the sock crept downward, emerging cuff first. When the cuff of the sock neared the pair on his feet, the match was confirmed by the width of the ribs and the yellow shade of white.

As was destined to happen, the sock fell to the pavement. I bent to retrieve it then wished I had not. With the sock in my hand I could not bring myself to enact whatever moves were necessary. I could not think of the right words to address him, nor the right gestures to accompany the words. I could think only of his embarrassment and my corresponding embarrassment and the unavoidable moment when together we would watch his feet, unmoving, in his tattered shoes.

COUNTLESS TIMES in my cleaning I have come across a sock, or an earring, or any other unpaired thing, stripped of value by the loss of its mate. Though, practically speaking, the thing is no less useful, could be paired with any other of its kind, there is a sense of incompleteness that cannot be undone. I hate to be the steward of these objects, neither lost nor found, neither broken nor repaired.

I clean from left to right and top to bottom because left to right is the order of the Western world. Without order, details are overlooked. The Japanese clean from right to left, an equal and opposite order. There is no harm in approaching results from a different direction. Cleaning does not thrill me, but there are moments of great relief, akin to exhilaration: a mirror's shine restored, a carpet refurbished to its nascent pile, a white floor revealed. Restore, refurbish, reveal. We think of cleanliness as a return to order when, in fact, it is a new and momentary order. When the results of cleaning can no longer be observed, it is time to stop.

E VERY PART OF THE COOP was born of something else. The coop itself is an old garden shed, the outdoor run is made from three wooden pallets found nesting in the rafters of the garage, the feed box is two pieces of plywood scrap held together with two-by-four scrap and topped with a spare ceramic knob from the cupboards in the kitchen. The nesting boxes are an old dollhouse belonging to Percy's ex-girlfriend.

What I know of Percy's ex-girlfriend could fit in a sherbet bowl. In the freezer she left a half gallon of orange sherbet, from which she had eaten one spoonful. When a year had passed and the sherbet remained in the same position as when I arrived, the details of its nutritious load facing outward, I opened the carton made soft by time. On the underside of the lid grew a thick colony of glittering crystals. The sherbet itself had been transformed by exposure to the cold air, had become some other thing entirely, made of gum and syrup and the color orange. All day long the neon clod in the sink inched toward the drain. Upon arriving there, it plugged the sink more effectively than the plug designed to do so ever had.

ABOUT THAT TIME, one year after moving in, I had found the old dollhouse in the madcap clutter of the garage. I called Helen upon my discovery.

"What would you do if you discovered a dollhouse in your boyfriend's garage?"

"Did you?" Helen asked.

"What would you do?"

"How big is it?"

"About six square feet."

"Are you asking if I want it?"

"No. I'm asking what it means."

"Why not ask Percy?"

"I can't ask him what it means before I know what it means."

Helen did not respond.

"Clearly his last girlfriend wanted to have children and left the dollhouse to symbolize the demise of their relationship."

"Or she forgot it."

I went straight to the couch to pry Percy from his busyness.

"A dollhouse?" he said. "Throw it away, unless you want it."

"I thought you said she didn't want children." He had told me this, had said he did not want to have a child with her because she had told him she did not want children. But here was a dollhouse placed right where he could see it, were it not for a particular blindness. His stance on children was to not want whatever his girlfriend did not want or, rather, to not want what she said she did not want, even if they were both wrong about it. I did not want to live with a man who could not think for himself, therefore he did not want me to live with him.

"Or you could leave it in the garage," he said.

I stayed up late into the night rearranging every cupboard in the kitchen. The next morning Percy took the sugar from its new spot on the shelf and noted the perfect alignment without a word.

"I want children," I said.

"Let's have children."

THIS MORNING a white-haired man who lives two doors down knocked on the front door bearing a crisp envelope. "I don't know if you remember me," he said. "I live in the red rambler, two houses down."

"Of course," I said. I would know him anywhere on account of his ring of hair, combed so carefully downward, and his never-changing stance, back bent, hands fixed out in front as if reaching for a tall weed.

"I would be happy to contribute five dollars if there is a way to quiet the chickens."

What did he have in mind?

"They sound hungry," he said.

The chickens are not hungry, have not been hungry a day in their lives, perhaps even a minute. The noise they made as he stood on our doorstep was for some other reason or, as I suspect, no reason at all. You can't keep a bird from singing, and it follows that you can't keep a chicken from sounding as a chicken does.

"I'll check on the chickens," I said. "Thanks for stopping by."

"It's good to get out and enjoy the sunshine," he said, though he returned home directly, where he had likely been waiting for weeks or more, envelope at the ready, for the last threat of ice to pass.

ASIDE FROM THE NOISE of the chickens, the morning was full of chirps and warbles and a faraway mechanical drone that may have been the emergence of the seven-year cicadas or a distant train laden with oil. Percy had taken to the field, meaning he had ridden the bus into town without destination. I opened wide the gate of the run and out scurried Darkness, her dovey babble sounding for all the world like a pressing question. She headed straight to the hostas to scratch and peck, throwing great heaps of mulch onto the suffering grass. I did not give the two missing chickens a thought, though if I had I might have concluded, with some measure of excitement, they were laying eggs as a good chicken does and awaited the fanfare of their self-appreciation. I sat on the edge of the garden, book in hand, to discourage the chickens from wreaking havoc on what had only begun to grow there.

I lifted my head to survey the yard, not reading so

much as enjoying the heft of the book and the cool shadow cast by it upon my legs. Our small yard holds a lifetime of amusement for the chickens and is the pinnacle of their existence. "Chicken heaven," I called it for years, though now I don't. The chickens fly just well enough to escape over the lowest section of the fence, a three-foot rise, but they do not know they can fly and therefore do not know they can escape, nor do they yearn for it.

Darkness was deep in the hostas, I could tell by the shushing of her body in the broad leaves and the crisp sound of torn paper as she left her mark. But where were the others? Chickens prefer to range free. This is why we pay so dearly for the eggs of such chickens, believing they have lived as they would choose to live, though the argument falls away quite soon after. I suddenly felt that something in the coop was amiss.

HELEN BELIEVES a grave feeling begets grave consequences. She has spoken to me of this belief on several occasions but not for some time, and I think she may never mention it again. In any case, it was clear my sudden sense of dread was not a suitable explanation for the scene I encountered upon entering the coop. The particulars of the tableau within had been set into motion long before I felt unease. My grave feeling was only the truth of the situation. Miss Hennepin County lay splayed for butcher, head twisted at the most improbable angle, as if beneath this lifeless chicken was another lifeless chicken to whom the head belonged. All around me the typical noises continued: the solitary buzz of a wasp, the dry rustle of a mouse darting from view, the twitter of a sparrow that had flown in through the opening to investigate and found no menace in the pile of rust-colored feathers, so began to eat the pellets of food plentiful on the floor.

As for Gloria, either she was traumatized or whatever had gotten Miss Hennepin County had gotten her too but treated her more kindly, then left her in the rightmost, rarely used nesting box, her head drawn deep into the shrug of her wings. From this exact posture turtles live to ages over a hundred years, but a bird does not wear it well. On a bird, the posture signifies defeat.

No trace was left of what had caused one death and one trauma in a confined space from which Darkness had emerged unscathed. The mystery allayed my shock and sadness. My first thought was the old man neighbor and his bid for silence.

. . .

THE HEFT OF HER BODY surprised me, and the inflexible flatness. Held aloft it was as if the ground continued to support her back and legs. Only her head flopped in accordance with gravity because, I was sure, her neck had been broken. I set her body on top of the green bin full of straw and retrieved my phone to call Percy. He said of course her neck was broken if she had died on her perch and fallen from such height at such an angle—I had stopped just short of imagining the chicken being wrung lifeless—and I should sit down and not think at all and he'd be right home.

When I emerged from the coop bearing the dead chicken, I found Rita with her scissors, cutting whichever lilacs she could reach from over the fence of our back neighbors' yard, from the bush that had once belonged to Cal and Lynn. "What a nice day," she said. Not long before it had been the truth, but in no time at all, a gulf had formed between us.

I sat with the chicken, out of sight, but I could not think of nothing. I thought instead of how I am sure of the chickens' safety only when they are in my arms, and sometimes not even then. And though the chickens do not prefer to be held, it wasn't only for me that I held her in my lap, cool and shapeless as she was; rather, some idea I had of what she needed from me.

Gloria spent two days in the nest box. She did not cluck or chortle, did not drink a drop, and her head could not be coaxed from its determined tuck with even the juiciest worm. But then, on the third day, as quickly as the shadow had overtaken our home, it lifted. As I scrubbed the kitchen floor I heard the particular timbre of Gloria's squawk announcing her comeback in excelsis.

DARKNESS is now the captain of this peppy squad, has always been the loudest chicken and has upped her personal racket as if to compensate for her insecurities. She is missing the left toe on her left side, so leans heavily, with her head cocked to the right to keep from tipping over completely. When the darkest eggs appear in the nest box, the racket is almost unbearable. The sharp bleats perforate the air of the entire neighborhood and pulse through me as if I am personally responsible. Before signing on the dotted line of our chicken permit application—the permit required the signature of all the neighbors within a block—each and every neighbor asked, pen poised, "Will you have a rooster?" They weren't concerned with the fornication of chickens on our property, though I can imagine this aspect of raising chickens to be, at turns, disturbing. The sheer frequency of the mount, for one thing, but also the polygamy, the incest, and the spurs of the rooster, used for mounting, which are occasionally, in the cases of greatest enthusiasm, the cause of a poor hen's demise. All of this aside, the neighbors wanted only to know if the chickens would make a racket. I answered their question: "No, we will not have a rooster." As proof, I cited the line of the permit explicitly forbidding a rooster on our property. But I knew nothing of the noise of hens, which turns out to be considerable, and of our two remaining hens, Darkness has the loudest mouth by far. Her mouth is also the largest. She pecks the ground as many as ten times before raising her head to swallow. Meanwhile, Gloria is up and down and up again, managing at most three pecks before tamping down whatever morsels she's unearthed. I have put behind me the notion of our neighbor as culprit, but if he was responsible, he had targeted the wrong chicken.

CHICKENS MOST LIKELY have no grasp of their status in the world, but perhaps they sense what they cannot know: the world is overrun with chickens. There are nineteen billion chickens in the world. The number is not exact on account of its steady rise. Chickens are popping out of eggs at a rate that cannot be calculated. To determine the actual population of chickens in the world would require such a collective pause in chewing we might as well orchestrate a moment of worldwide silence. Somehow, despite all the gnawing of white meat, there are also incalculable eggs. Given the acceleration of hatching chickens and shoveling eggs, we will have nothing left to feed the chickens but the eggs they have just laid.

I have never once been attacked by a chicken as I took an egg from its resting place. Rarely do I collect an egg while a chicken sits upon it, and then only with the dustpan as my trusty shield. On several occasions Gloria tried to attack me, when she was broody, but at all other times the chickens relinquish their eggs without a backward glance. There is no explanation for the nonchalance with which a chicken leaves a gleaming egg in a round of hay prodded into a perfect circle by the hen's own crooked feet, unless chickens have somehow perceived strength in their numbers. Never mind that they exist in such multitude for the sole purpose of being dispensed with as quickly as possible. I have always considered a chicken to have no capacity for hope, but perhaps a chicken lacks only a reason.

PERCY RECEIVED A LETTER from the prestigious university. The letter states that he will soon receive another letter with the details of its decision. We have waited for a decision, and now we have received a letter confirming our wait. The letter says nothing, but says so on expensive paper. When held to the light there is proof of the university and its prestige. Percy claims a letter that says nothing means something. I think this is true only if the letter has a postscript, in which case the postscript says everything. P.S., this letter has none. Percy is confident the delay of the news is the best news possible. If in fact an offer is forthcoming, the additional wait suggests tight circles are expanding outward to consolidate funds on our behalf. As a rule, my husband creates certainty where it does not exist.

JOHNSON SMILED when he saw the chickens. "He's happy to see you," Helen said. Johnson paid me no mind. He followed the black chicken and was followed by the silver. The woman who watches Johnson in the mornings has come down with strep throat for the third time this year and I agreed to watch Johnson in her stead. In the two months since I had seen him last, he had learned to walk, and I could tell it was the source of great satisfaction. His pride had perhaps come into being for the very occasion of walking. "I don't care what he does as long as he wears his hat," Helen said.

Johnson and I are an even match: my steps are longer but he takes so many. We passed an hour this way, me at his heels as he followed every whim and bird. He wanted to hug a chicken and was possibly saying so out loud. Johnson's noises intrigue the chickens, have a similar squawking quality and no doubt comprise the same basic instincts, prompting the chickens to respond in kind. The conversation between them always seems of great importance and also great civility, what with the polite distance maintained at all times (despite Johnson's advances), heads cocked on either side in the guise of good listening and, because the chickens are positioned to look Johnson directly in the eye, the semblance of utmost respect.

EACH SOUND a chicken makes has meaning. No one knows if these sounds contain information, like our words, or if the sounds of a chicken merely provoke action in the world at large. If at first these seem like the same thing, consider a scream. A scream provokes action without specific information. The specifics prove unimportant. Whatever else a scream aims to accomplish, it gets attention. The same is true of the scream of a chicken, harsh and rising. It is safe to assume that a scream of some form was a precursor to every human language, just as every known human language uses high, soft sounds to comfort a baby. A chicken also uses these high, soft sounds to comfort her young, but because the lives of chickens have evolved toward a separation of hens and chicks, more and more chickens do not learn this language, never hear it, nor use it. At some point, the motherese of chickens will cease to exist, leaving the world no different.

While there is not agreement on the subject of chickens and words, there is agreement that chickens speak only of the here and now. A chicken does not speak of the day before. A chicken does not speak of tomorrow. A chicken speaks of this moment. I see this. I feel this. This is all there is.

It stands to reason, then, that the sounds of a chicken are few, here and now accounting for so much of what a chicken has to say. The sounds do not misrepresent, are instead like a finger pointing, over and over. Words have only ever complicated things. As I watched Johnson trample the hostas, touching each thing and gabbling in turn, I thought he and the chickens might understand each other completely.

Eventually, Johnson tired of the chickens or was just plain tired. He began to cry. I needed a word he would know and like. "Nap," I said, and his crying turned to screaming. I tucked him beneath my arm as I had learned to do, but he began to kick, and, anyway, he was too long now to hold with ease. I lowered him to the ground and the kicking did not become running, as I would have expected, but instead a violent assault on the grass, which looked quite exhausting and must have been, after which he rolled over three times to arrive at the upturned earth where the chickens bathed. "Ice cream," I said.

. . .

HIS LIP CURLED in a snarl of anticipation as he ate each bite, the same way Helen's lip curls before speaking. I can always tell when Helen has made up her mind to say something and has stopped listening altogether. Each time Percy and I visit his mother, I discover a new resemblance between them. Not new at all, but previously unseen, exposed by some random sequence of words or action. I am always startled by these chance encounters with the fact that she is his mother—shared philosophy of toxic debt, dishtowel drying on the cupboard door, laughter as substitute for feeling. Whether or not I love Percy's mother, I understand her, and surely the two become one at some point down the road, whereas Percy does not understand her but loves her with the blind ferocity of habit.

I OPEN THE GATE of the outdoor run each morning to let the chickens roam free. The blossoms of the spirea have burst into tufts of white, but the chickens pay them no mind, whereas a late daffodil, having unfurled overnight—white also, with a yellow center—is readily trounced to the ground.

The chickens look fat. I have never before considered our chickens fat, not when the mailman suggested it years ago, nor in March when I discovered I had been feeding the chickens the equivalent of 50 percent Twinkies. I have not thought of the Twinkies for weeks on end and am surprised now, upon thinking of it, to find the feeling of treachery so close at hand.

I DID NOT DRIVE ten miles to the Farm and Fleet off Highway 62 for feed. Because our chickens are fat, I drove twenty miles in the opposite direction to buy organic feed from a small shop in St. Paul called "The Egg and I."

The man who owns the shop has fine features and slender hands. I hope this has something to do with his propensity for organic food. The man inquired about my chickens and their habits and my concerns about both. He was not surprised by anything I told him because, he said, today's chickens grow twice as big in half the time.

"Would you like the standard-size pellets or the large ones?" he asked.

"Does it matter?"

"The large pellets make less dust and are easy to clean up."

"I'll take those."

"Your chickens might not eat them. Most chickens find the large pellets hard to swallow."

I have no reason to believe our chickens have bigger mouths or larger gullets or are generally exceptional when compared with other chickens. "The small ones then," I said.

"I recommend the small ones."

A sign taped to a glass tank read FREE CHICK WITH PURCHASE OF FEED. The fine fur of the chicks' feathered bodies moved as a single orange cloud beneath the heat of the red light. I did not want a free chick, nor could I afford one, though I would have liked to hold one, to cup the tiny charm of its heart against my thin sweater.

A woman waited at the counter as her young son emptied his pockets of change. He wanted a chick and the promotion made it possible to buy a small bag of feed instead. Children do not know that buying a chick is just the beginning. Parents, if this idea occurs to them at all, underestimate the extent of it, especially if they have never cared for animals themselves or if they are living in debt, even more so if they come from a long line of similar circumstances.

Behind the counter, the owner parted his lips in preparation for accepting whatever short amount of change was spread before him. The boy made four pillars of the coins, and the mother saw here an opportunity for teaching or learning or distraction from the fact that she was about to become the owner of another life, however small, so she gave a brief lesson in quarters and dimes, all of which I did not mind. I even found a little happiness in the young boy's excitement. The mother was quite a good teacher. I felt that I also was learning something, though I could not have said what, as she shuffled coins on the counter like a bit of magic. The boy would surely leave with a chicken and he seemed to understand this through his solemn nodding.

THE BOY LEFT with his chick, the runt of the litter, in a box lined with the particular bedding most suitable to chicks, along with the smallest sack of the smallest pellets and a bottle of drops and a package of wipes for the chick's bottom, having chosen a chick with a pasty butt, though his mother had urged him otherwise. The boy paid four dollars and seventy-two cents for the free chick and its trappings, and his mother paid thirty dollars more. "Three drops a day in fresh water," the man reminded, laying a grave hand on the boy's shoulder as he escorted him to the door.

"I'VE NEVER USED drops in the water," I said to the man.

"Most people use vinegar. That's what I recommend."

"I've never put anything in the water."

"You must have hardy chickens."

The man rang up three bags of standard-size organic pellets for a total of ninety-nine dollars and change.

I LEFT THE ORGANIC FEED piled high in the trunk and went straight to the coop. In the kitchen, I scoured the jug inside and out. When I had finished my scrubbing, the sponge bore a brilliant streak of green. From beneath the sink I took the gallon of white vinegar and doctored the water in the chickens' jug. All the while the chickens went about their business. Darkness rummaged around in the low barbs of the youngest hostas. Gloria bathed in a patch of dirt she had cleared from under a ragged black mat of last year's leaves. The shaggy pile sat beside her like a chicken of poor design. In the midst of their daily activity, the chickens did not look fat at all.

THREE BAGS OF FEED might last two months. It depends on how much goes to waste; I expect plenty. Last spring the chickens stopped laying completely and not an egg was laid for two months straight. At the start of the dry spell the chickens were molting. Feathers of every shape and color littered the coop: proud russet shafts, soft gray underfeathers, white wisps of down, stiff bristles brushed with orange, and the occasional black-bearded feather with a glint of green. All about the yard feathers floated on air, often via a breeze so slight only a feather skirting the ground confirmed it. After the molting had run its course, after the feathers had been swept into quivering piles and placed on the compost, after the wind had taken all it wanted, still the chickens did not lay. They ate and they drank and they carried on as usual while their calcium and proteins amassed in some ethereal place. The dry spell went on and on, like a battle of wills between them, though I have never otherwise considered chickens to possess will or to exercise it in any way. We bought inferior eggs by the dozen: no heft, no character, wan yolks, whites full of water, thin blah shells, no flavor at all, though the flavor I speak of is not egg exactly. Then, finally, Gloria laid an egg on the cement walkway leading to the house. This had never before happened and never has since. The egg lay on the concrete, whole and fragile and glowing ever so slightly in the warmth of the sun. The chickens gathered around it, squawking with awed ferocity. From then on the chickens laid consistently, but much less than before. If this spring is anything like the last, each egg will be worth its weight in gold.

THE NIGHT FREIGHT rumbled past as I thought of the boy and his doomed chick. Would he feed her enough? Would he feed her too much? Would he feed her the gummy candy that looks like a worm and behaves more or less in the same manner? Would his mother know what to do— she would not—but would she learn? Would she teach him with her enchanting gestures? Would she check his work or would she let him be? Would she tuck the chick into a black pocket of her mind where all things die? When I was young, I pretended to do everything I was told but I did not do any of it. I did not brush my teeth; I wiped them with the sleeve of my shirt. I did not do my homework; I placed stickers in neat rows on the back side of my closet door. Would the boy read the label of the dropper-topped bottle? Could he read? Would he love her? Would he sleep alongside her in his stifling bed?

T HE FANCY PELLETS disappear in a cloud of their own making. Organic feed creates more dust than its counterpart, is so conducive to digestion that it begins to metabolize in midair, free-floating for minutes before settling on every horizontal plane. Within five days, the coop was shrouded in a thick batting of powdered protein and B vitamins. The thin wire of the chicken fencing bore a fine silt of dust resting on every base edge of its six-sided mesh.

The sound of the new pellets, a drumroll of grain on tin, is a different sound, a lower tone due to the increased volume of each pellet. Despite the pellets being standard-size pellets for average chickens, I am not sure the chickens can swallow them. The chickens are drawn to the tinny rattle of new food but only nose the pellets from the feeder to the floor, where the dense pebbles of grain lend traction amid the straw and dirt and feathers and poop, and the whole of it over time is woven by the needles of pronged feet into a carpet of the highest nutritive value.

. . .

WHEN I FIRST LEARNED that chickens don't have teeth I realized I had known it all along. I can picture the teeth of a cat or a dog or a horse in vivid detail. I can even recall a tooth I once encountered on a string around young Katherine's neck, who claimed the tooth was that of a cow, and because the tooth was large, frighteningly so, and stained a grassy green, I believed her. Whereas I cannot imagine the teeth of a chicken. What a terrifying thought, that busy beak full of chompers.

In lieu of teeth, chickens chew their food in a special stomach full of rocks. A pellet of food must travel from beak to throat to stomach through all manner of snug tunnels and soft caverns without being chewed, which is why swallowing a large pellet presents a problem. A chicken is not born with a stomach full of rocks. The rocks must be eaten. The rocks are a nonnegotiable part of a chicken's diet. I feed the chickens rocks in a separate smaller feeder alongside their food. The rocks come from a zip-top bag of rocks purchased in the poultry section of Farm and Fleet and do not differ from natural rocks in any discernible way. The rocks, once eaten, are churned in the caustic juices of the stomach where the organic pellets, if any, hiss and fizz, along with beetles and worms and especially scratch grains, every piece of kibble and otherwise transformed into a sour slurry. Even the rocks themselves weaken and break apart, becoming the tart paste that passes like wet sand through the remaining tubes and vents of a chicken. Because the rocks of the stomach do not last forever, a finicky chicken that eschews pellets of all sizes continues to eat rocks. The world is full of such mysteries, perhaps significant, perhaps not.

P ERCY'S NEW BOOK is expected to be received favorably in the world at large because piece by piece it already has been. His upcoming book details, among other trivialities, his take on no free lunch. He embraces sleep and a late breakfast, which eliminates the need for lunch. Percy is passionate about eliminating the need for lunch. This is yet another way his worldview corroborates trends worldwide. Lunch is out of fashion, or, rather, breakfast is the new lunch.

Many professors teach Percy's books to their classes. This guarantees sales but discourages readership. In addition to the guarantee of classroom sales, there is buzz among experts that, according to cycles preordained and charted throughout history, it is once again time for a boring book to become popular. The success of Percy's previous books stands as point of proof on this upward trajectory. In the last month alone, Percy has been contacted by a university (not prestigious), two panels, a forum, and a women's magazine. He is bearing up well under the scrutiny, though he has enrolled in an online course to access his inner baritone.

THE SECOND LETTER ARRIVED two weeks after the first. Percy has been offered the job of associate professor on the tenure track, and the dean of the School of Economics is eager to show his eagerness. The letter invited Percy to visit as soon as possible. He left the following morning in high spirits. Not only was the letter studded with praise, but Percy himself had predicted the offer, suggesting that his judgment is, for the time being, still in line with the mechanics of the world. His instincts told him to catch a flight the next morning to further his good standing and to bring with him a basket of cheese.

Percy's research is not isolating; rather, it consists primarily of living life as he wants to live it. Not long after we married, Helen asked me if it bothered me, the possibility that Percy had married me as a kind of personal experiment. This thought had never occurred to me, but, of course, it is one way to look at our relationship and not a wrong way. I married him for the same reason, if she wanted to be reductive about it. I wanted to see if my impression of Percy, of who he is, had been more or less right all along. I hoped my life would be better with him in it, but only time would tell.

If Percy had married me to write a treatise on marriage, he would have written it by now. Sometimes I do question my role in his life and the likelihood of exhausting it. At the point where I become an uninteresting subject to him, or him to me, will the whole thing fall apart?

IT WAS PERCY who told Helen the baby had died because I could not say the words out loud, or I could not stand to hear the words all over again. Percy accepted the task dutifully, did not flinch or ask how to go about it. I don't know what he told Helen, whether he referred to me or to us, or if he provided a theory, as he is never without one. It was only months later that I wanted to know his version of it. The words he had chosen, and his bearing, seemed to offer a specific glimpse of him that had otherwise escaped me. By then it seemed too late to ask.

When I next saw Helen, on our doorstep clutching flowers, she hugged me and said, "I'm so sorry." That was all she said, dear Helen, who errs most often on the side of talking. She brought the flowers to the kitchen, removed the plastic wrapper, and left the towering arrangement in a glass of water on the counter there.

THE BABY had been due on the last day in September, and though such dates are not exact, I still think of it as the day she was not born. Summer of that year was rainy at first and dry for weeks after, so that, by the end of September, the trees were colorful beyond reckoning. My thoughts then were organized around a central principle that the baby was supposed to have happened and the miscarriage was not, was the aberration that could not be explained. According to this, the fine color of autumn was meant for us.

The last day of September came and went like any other, but first, in the wee hours of the morning, an idea occurred to me. I slipped from the bed, silent, and down the stairs. I had seen that Percy's notebooks were dated like a journal and I was suddenly filled with an urge to know if his notes bore any reference to the day's significance. I found his notebook where I thought I might, open to the empty page of October 1. The page behind that was missing. If there had been a note on the date the baby was due, it was gone now. Nothing he might have written could have hurt me more than to know he had torn this page so carefully as to leave no trace of it. Back in bed, I touched his lips with my finger in the hope that I would wake him, but he continued to sleep.

Throughout the morning he tended to me in the usual ways—poured my coffee before his; cleared my plate from the table, onto which he brushed a crumb from the table's edge; looked up from his work to see me and smiled—all of his actions made compelling somehow by my noticing each and every one.

S EVERAL MONTHS after the news of my miscarriage, Helen called me with the suggestion of a gift. She had learned of a woman who led private psychic tours of the permanent collection of the Minneapolis Institute of Art. One of Helen's realtor friends had taken a psychic art tour to vanquish her infertility, and Helen wanted to pay for my first session. As Helen spoke, it was clear she had not practiced the delivery of her speech, and the word "infertility," though it might have been avoided with sufficient foresight, caught her quite off guard. The word did not bother me because, at the time of her suggestion, I believed myself to be pregnant again. Helen assured me that even if I did not put stock in the practice, my energy could be tapped and interpreted and there would be results. "At the very least it will be an experience," she said.

I agreed to the session because I could not express the extent of my skepticism without hurting Helen's feelings and, also, I had all the time in the world. I had quit cleaning houses soon after losing the baby on a sudden conviction that the cleaning itself—the products or the vigor—was preventing me from having a baby. The next available appointment with the spiritual art dealer was five weeks out. Helen declared the delay good fortune, because the psychic was in high demand, indicating her credibility, whereas I felt the futility of the endeavor had been compounded. If I was in fact pregnant, those five weeks would span the time in which the nubs of eyes, lungs, and heart distinguish themselves. Any benefit that could be derived from the psychic tour, despite my doubts, would have no effect on the formation of the nubs or what grew from them.

BY THE TIME I met the spiritual art dealer, I knew I was not again pregnant. The test's 99.7 percent surety made me more certain of not being pregnant than I was of anything else in my life.

The psychic stood like a statue in the lobby of the museum. Her back was straight and her arms outstretched as if her whole purpose in standing there was to maximize the drape of her many purple garments. I knew she was the right woman because I could sense that she knew I was the right woman. The psychic art dealer took my hands in hers, thus confirming her identity. She placed a velvet scarf from around her neck over my eyes and knotted it behind my head. She did not tell me her name because, I suppose, she knew I did not care to know. The scarf smelled like coffee, and it seemed to me this woman, a mysterious woman with such remarkable posture, should have smelled like something else, something less ordinary, and the fact that she smelled like plain old coffee shook my faith in her. I was briefly overwhelmed with disappointment. Until the moment of disappointment, I had not realized I had placed any faith in her at all. I had told myself I was meeting this woman for Helen's sake, but it turned out I hoped the woman could help me.

She guided me step by step up ten broad stairs and across the smooth stone landing. The wooden heels of my shoes knocked loudly on the marble floor. Her shoes, if she wore them, made no sound at all. I could not be sure her hand remained on my elbow; I could not feel its presence there. A draft of air suggested I had arrived in a great open space, and I stopped only out of worry for what lay ahead, not out of spiritual impulse, unless worry itself could be considered one. I suppose what I had learned was that it could be. I was suddenly certainly alone.

The psychic art dealer left me standing in front of a painting of a woman smoking a cigarette. It was not the first time I had seen this painting. Percy and I had once visited the museum before we were engaged. There was, during the months leading up to our engagement, a feeling that the spell of love we were under was as fragile as it had ever been. This is true of all love in the months leading up to engagement. They are the most fragile months because feeling must be transformed into protocol. To sign one's name at the bottom of one's present feelings in the hope that the feelings persist is counter to all life experience. In addition, many relationships cannot withstand the slog of paperwork that marriage entails, nor should they.

On this earlier visit, the painting of the smoking woman had captured my attention. The smoking woman sits, spine straight, face placid but not quite void of emotion. In her smoking, I saw a contentment beyond any I had experienced, both a contentment derived from the act of smoking and a confidence in the act itself. If the painting is in fact a portrait, which it most likely is, the woman no doubt smoked a good number of cigarettes as the painting progressed, all with great confidence and satisfaction, or, at the very least, on average with both contentment and confidence, and the average, which approximates truth, had been immortalized as such.

As Percy ambled ahead, I stood to scrutinize the painting, drawing all of these conclusions, which did not change the very first impression the painting had given me.

"Have you ever wanted to be a smoker?" I asked Percy.

"Why do you ask?"

"The painting of the smoking woman."

"What woman?"

I led him back to the painting. He had not seen it, though we had walked the same path.

"Why would smoking even occur to you?"

"Because of the effect it has on her."

"The addiction?"

"The contentment."

"Do you know what that's called?"

"Contentment or addiction?"

"When the relief from the thing is the thing itself."

"I don't want to know."

Next to the smoking woman was a painting of a sailboat. There was no line of horizon where the water met the sky. The gray blue of the water faded into the blue gray of the sky, and somewhere within this bluer gray there was a thin gray cloud confirming it. "I have always wanted to learn how to sail," Percy said. He placed his arm around me and squeezed my shoulder.

UPON SEEING THE PAINTING for the second time, delivered to that very spot by the hands of the psychic art dealer, I could not have been more surprised. The painting so obviously depicted grief. Or rather, the painting captured a specific instance of grief. What I had earlier thought to be confidence was in fact desperation; what I had taken for

contentment was relief. The cigarette was not mere pleasure or habit—its orange embers were the very embodi-
ment of hope. If the painting is in fact a portrait, and I
think it must be, the smoking woman must have sat there
in her sadness for quite some time.

I T SOUNDED Like a Freight Train" was the headline in *The North Star*. Percy had not been gone an hour when the tornado hit. He later claimed to have seen the dark mass of wind and rain, tail spinning, as his plane flew west.

I had driven Percy to the airport. On the way home, from the stoplight at Dowling, I watched as the strip of light between the trees and the black clouds shrank into a thin line. Far on the horizon a toy tree floated up and away in the direction of Fridley. I did not wait for the light to turn green.

Of course the chickens had acted strange. They had seemed desperate to prevent Percy's departure, pacing back and forth along the mesh of the outdoor run, whereas the chickens do not typically care one lick about Percy's comings or goings. To attribute such strangeness to a national weather event would never have occurred to me. Darkness in particular had clawed at the gate as we hurried to the car. The crazed look in her eye had seemed at the time quite ordinary.

. . .

I SAT BENEATH the stairs in the basement with Gloria tucked in the nest of my folded legs, where she did not seem especially at home. I could not help but think that if I were a spider, I would be here, too. The moment I set Gloria free, she began exploring every inch of the basement, happily harvesting I don't care to know what.

The wind became louder and louder until my whole body hummed with the force of it. I could not think of it as noise at all but, rather, a silence full of pain in my head. A brutal crash shook the house. The lights went out and I thought of Darkness. Her leg had brushed my hand as she blew the length of the backyard, where she now roamed loose beneath the dying maple or was pinned to the fence in the gale or, if she had any sense at all, cowered beneath the stairs of the back landing, though I have heard of nails plucked from boards and placed elsewhere by the sheer velocity of such winds, have heard even of twigs acting in this manner, the wind providing in force of speed what the twig lacks in every other respect. The maple can hardly weather a plain day, bends low over the house on account of every major limb on the opposite side having fallen away and, despite the spring growth on its branches, bears a crown of crisp leaves that rattle like a dangerous animal camouflaged above. And now this.

When the wind died suddenly, all that remained of the sound was the familiar wail of the warning provided by the city should a tornado transpire. The first Wednesday of every month for as long as anyone can remember, the system has been tested, never employed for any purpose beyond testing, so that now, upon hearing it, I thought only that it must be the first Wednesday in May.

IT IS UNORIGINAL to liken a tornado to a freight train, compounded in our neighborhood by the fact that a train is always present. Still, it is a definitive truth that these sounds are the same sound, one natural, one not. A tornado in our neighborhood poses an additional threat for exactly this reason: the dull roar that warns of disaster is also the sound of life here. When the storm hit, the people of the neighborhood were out and about, up to their usual business or their usual lack thereof. The tornado bounced like a spring over the neighborhood, sending a confetti of shingles into the air and touching down three times: first near the school, shucking the young fruit trees of their blossoms; again over the pond in Webber Park, where the ducks have not yet returned; and finally on top of the cafe on the corner of Forty-second and Lyndale, robbing a billboard of its message in fleshy strips and allowing the owner of the always failing cafe to close its doors for good, I imagine with a great sigh of relief.

It was a miracle no one was hurt, given the number of trees that toppled in Webber Park, the park where everything happens, sordid and otherwise, and everyone goes. Everyone in the park for the minute it lasted watched the giant trees—all oaks aged seventy years or more—float up from the ground and dance a tarantella across the sky as the wind moved through them. The trees landed on their sides and continued to live, lengthwise, until the city came to cut them and chip them and cart them away.

N OT ONLY did the maple survive the storm, it seemed taller. The speckled shadow of its young leaves landed on the grass below, and in that shadow lay a still dark smudge. If I had not been intent on the tree's collapse, I might never have found Darkness there, perched on a branch near the top, her silhouette flat against the new blue sky. I suppose the same wind that brought her high might also have brought her low, but the wind had died first.

The chicken made no move to suggest she was keen on returning to the world beneath her. I could not imagine how to retrieve her, but, for a moment, my excitement in her safety, in her unlikely perch so high in the sky, prevented me from worry. I felt suddenly, and with a conviction that eclipsed all experience, that the chickens were invincible, that luck had turned upside down in our favor and nothing in the world could thwart the lives of the two remaining chickens.

. . .

I THREW TWO HANDFULS of corn high in the air and listened as the pieces scattered about. Not a kernel reached Darkness at the top of the tree. If she watched me, there was no sign of it. Gloria hurried to eat the corn all around me. There must be something of substance in the tree itself, I thought, a tree so riddled with holes. But I knew a chicken could not live long without water. Beneath a cloudless sky, perhaps a day.

From the garage I fetched the ladder, which I've always considered to be antique on account of its poor condition. Two of the six steps have been replaced with sturdy dowels and the looseness of the remaining joints suggests why. Against the maple, the ladder was only a toy, did not reach half the distance I had hoped. But I could see how I might craft the remaining section of trunk into a ladder of its own by nailing pieces of wood as footholds to the lowest branch. From there I could reach the only major limb and, if I was able to scoot across it and raise my arms above my head, pluck the chicken from the utmost branch. Thus, I would deliver the chicken to safety, or perhaps she would fly into my arms as I made my way to her.

I gathered three planks of wood from a pile of scrap, the jam jar full of nails, and a hammer. The shifting of the ladder did not dissuade me as I climbed to the topmost step with a row of nails between my teeth. The first nail pierced the plank with ease and punctured the tree with two more taps of the hammer. And so on, until three boards were fixed solidly above me. My hands grasped the highest plank and then my feet refused to do their part, were stuck to the ladder not with fear exactly, but something more like common sense. As I looked downward from the dizzying, albeit modest, height, I had to agree. It was a child's plan, and even as a child I had not climbed trees.

I left the ladder flush with the tree so that Darkness would know she was not forgotten. I vowed that when morning came I would knock on every door in the neighborhood until I found the tallest ladder. It was just the kind of thing I would have asked Percy to do for me. As the sun began to set, I found it hard to believe he had been here this same day. Whatever I told him of the storm would be all he knew of it, the tree a grand perch now against the golden sky.

I WOKE to the alarm of a backward-moving utility truck. On the bed beside me was the hammer, and just outside the bedroom window rose the hydraulic lift of the electric crew, one man in the basket and two in the truck below, like a fleet of angels in shocking yellow dress. I knew in an instant the truck was the answer, so easily could the roving limb swing over the fence and within reach of the tree, if the men in vests could only be persuaded to grab a chicken.

I threw open the window. Amid the sprawl of the old parkway trees, the man in the truck's basket looked like a sprite, small and of the trees themselves. I swallowed a thick knot in my throat. "Please," I said, "a chicken is stuck in the top of that tree." I pointed out the window past a dangling wire. "Can you please help me?"

The arm of the truck swung near and the man became quite of this world. His voice was gruff as he explained he could not pull an animal from a tree for liability reasons. But I must have looked as desperate as I felt and, also, the hammer was in my hand.

"I could scare her down if you have a baseball," he said. "Course, if you have a hose, you could spray her down yourself."

We did not have a baseball, so I brought the roundest apple I could find. When I stepped out the back door, he was already waiting there, five feet above the fence. The apple reached him with my first toss, and he caught it in the palm of his hand with a slap. He looked long at the apple, but did not scoff, and placed his fingers just so on the apple's skin. The top of the tree was still some ways above him but not far to throw an apple. He shielded his eyes with his free hand and pulled back the other, and the hope that filled me was a giddy, greedy hope, that a thing I wanted should be so easily accomplished.

"Where is she?" he said.

The branch was empty. She was nowhere to be seen in the sparse green and there was no place in the tree for a chicken to hide.

"She was right here," I said. Not even the wind moved the tree's young leaves.

"All righty then," the man replied, and whether it was he who controlled the lift or the men in the truck itself, he sailed off without warning to another wind-torn wire.

DARKNESS WAS GONE. Not beneath the stairs, not in the hostas, not hovering just outside the closed gate of the coop, behind which Gloria stood distant watch over the garden like a member of the Secret Service, eyes unblinking. I heard a dull thud and could not bear to look. I turned to Gloria instead. She scratched at the gate with her crooked toes.

The thud had come from high above, though I cannot say how I knew this. Mightn't a thud have come from any which way? I scanned the yard from fence to fence and walked its perimeter with my eyes to the ground.

Just barely did I note the grass splayed sideways from the impact. At the edge of the hostas, in many pieces but mostly two, lay the parts of a broken apple.

Gloria showed no interest in the apple. She was intent on the garden, where nothing was as sweet and ready as the mess at my feet. The garden had not suffered a bit from the storm. The young lettuce stood one inch off the ground in tight green frills, the kale still haughty and tender. I opened the gate of the coop with an unfamiliar sense that the chicken knew something I did not. Gloria hurried toward the garden and straight into the low green fence surrounding it. Trapped as she was, I could see the direction of her attention, a ruddy fungus sprouting from the soil between two stalks of kale. There Darkness lay, so deep in the soil the red bloom of her comb sat even with the ground like a thing of its own. The comb shivered slightly and I knew she was alive. Beak-deep, eyes heavy, it seemed nothing would move her. I eased Gloria from one side to the other of the low green fence. The chicken did not think my gesture strange, though it was counter to any I had made before. Without pause she moved toward the patch of sun where Darkness lay and began to dig and kept on digging until they were nested side by side. All day long the chickens hovered in their garden hole as every pulse and tremor of the world below passed through them.

G ROVELAND GARDEN is the style of house that looks like a face, with windows for eyes, and a door for a mouth, and a lamp above the door that does not look like a nose until you've seen the face and then cannot be thought of as anything else. It's a friendly-looking house. The kind of house I wanted when I was a child and the kind of house I would have wanted for my own children. It seems impossible that such a house could exist without children in it of any kind, but on the inside all traces of past life have been removed, save for grime on the walls that stops abruptly at a certain height, and smudges around the switch plates, and, everywhere on the floor, the prints of countless sets of shoes, and, in one room only, on the ceiling, among the scat of fly and moth, bits of yellow putty on the rough surface where something was stuck not long ago, some childish thing, no doubt, like a set of stars that glows green in the dark; the putty is still pliant, though not easy to remove. From the bulb in the closet hangs a length of cotton string tied to a purple bead. The closet is painted purple, as is the inside of the closet door. The room must also have been purple at one time, I can tell, because the new paint job was not an especially careful one.

I clean in order to make a house seem as new as possible. Newness, and therefore cleanliness, is an optimistic state. Helen has told me that houses are bought from the heart. We buy a house for the life we want, not the life we have. I suppose she meant to warn me that I might still buy the house I wanted as a child or the house I wanted for my children. But there's nothing to stop a purple bead tied with cotton string from unraveling the whole pretty picture.

WE HAVE MISAPPROPRIATED the problem of dirt, though the solution remains the same. The problem with dirt these days is largely one of aesthetics—the presence of dirt does not align with the popular idea of what is beautiful. Whereas the problem with dirt for our ancestors was one of survival. The dirt of our ancestors was disease because the disease of our ancestors was natural. Modern disease is far more complicated.

An outbreak of bird flu has been discovered in the area among the population of wild birds. "Outbreak" is a misnomer. It is a comfort to think the flu has suddenly appeared, has in fact broken out of containment, when in reality no flu has ever been contained. The flu is always present, always all around us, though we note only the flu we see, meaning the signs of flu we recognize, most often the ones we feel or those complained of by others. This is perhaps why the nature of complaint is repellent, because to distance oneself from it was once, and may still be, a boon to survival.

The bird flu is causing quite a stir in the neighborhood. I would know nothing about it, were it not for the email chain bearing always the subject line: "What is happening in Camden neighborhood?" Percy has belonged to the Camden email group for longer than I have known him, and I expect he will go on receiving these emails forever, no matter where we live. The emails serve more or less as a fleet of field reporters for his ongoing research on community. I have not joined the chain because I would rather not know the goings-on of our neighborhood, though there is no opting out of the occasional glimpse of a neighbor mowing without a shirt. The emails are a grab bag of panic and misfortune with a rare bright spot: a neighbor claims a hobo has taken up residence in her giant oak; a Christian fish gone missing from a Buick on Irving; the parkway smells like butterscotch since the construction began, don't you think? Percy reads aloud the emails he finds amusing and also those pertaining directly to us. He has shared that "birds are getting the flu all over, putting ALL BIRDS at risk, who knows, maybe even people." Because the lock on caps seemed to be for our benefit, Percy assured the group at large that we monitor the chickens daily. Of course we watch the chickens. We cannot help but watch them, being as they are an endless source of entertainment and worry. But what exactly are we looking for?

I WATCH THE COMBS of the chickens for the telltale signs of bird flu. I have only just learned the signs: unusual droopiness and color. No specific color of comb indicates flu in chickens; only a change in the comb's color suggests flu, and because I did not note the color precisely before the outbreak, my worry has no basis. Gloria's comb is the exact powdered red of a fresh stick of gum, whereas Darkness's comb has the waxy pallor of a plastic toy left too long in the sun. The chickens' combs seem not red enough, but perhaps as red as they have ever been. I know the chickens could be healthier, what with the diet of scratch grains for years on end and the lack of a sprawling field to run in, but it seems to me the chickens are not less healthy than before, and either way, what can we do? Each morning I step outside to check on the chickens, but I do not open the door of the coop before thinking, please, please, let the chickens be safe, as if a late plea for their safety might wash away the cross of the plague.

. . .

EARLY IN THE MORNING there was a knock on the door. It was our old man neighbor, the same man who had requested the silence of our chickens not two months before. "I don't know if you remember me," he said.

"Of course I do, the red rambler."

"I came to tell you the phone tree's talking," he said. "My phone's been ringing off the hook." I pictured a wooden box nailed to the wall with two breasty bells a-ringing. Did Percy know about this grand old talking tree, and if so, why didn't he join it?

"The bird flu's got us all worried," the old man said. "How are your birds?"

"The chickens are fine. We keep a close eye on them," I said. I could tell by the way his mouth retained the shape of his next word that he had not yet said what he came to say. The plucky warble of the chickens reached us from behind the house, and I was suddenly certain the old man had come to condemn the chickens on behalf of the whole neighborhood.

"Be that as it may," he said, "the biggest danger to your birds are the wild ones. We've all agreed to stop feeding them till it's over."

"All?"

"The whole tree's agreed. That's every feeder in the neighborhood."

"Well, thank you," I said.

He turned to leave but did not. The morning chorus of the chickens crescendoed. Though I cannot always tell which chicken crows, I could tell on this morning, from the interval of sound, that there were two of them. Having just laid an egg, the noise of a chicken is that of surprise—an exponential noise because the noise of surprise is a surprise also. Thus the mushroom cloud of surprised noise that announces the arrival of new eggs in the world, first thing in the morning.

He turned again to face me. "Okay then," he said. "It's supposed to be a halfway decent day." Then he stepped with care in his thick-soled shoes, one stair at a time and down our front walk, onto the sidewalk and two doors down, to his own front door, where he checked for the mail that had not been delivered and disappeared inside the house.

T HE BACK LANDING is an ideal spot for watching chickens. At the foot of the landing lies a crude patchwork of broad, flat stones. Here sits a gas grill, two of its four wheels propped on a piece of wood scrap to level the cooking surface in order to prevent seared fat from dripping always into the back left corner. On a hot day Darkness prefers a particular cool stone in the shadow of the grill. Today is warm enough for the chickens to seek shade, whereas yesterday was cool and the chickens did not set foot outside the sunshine. In the evening I had found both chickens buried belly-deep near the compost in the last spot of sun.

Darkness lies so near to where I sit that I could rest my feet on her body, as if she were a tufted pillow. On her bed of flat stone, she busies herself picking mites and dander from her feathers and skin. Her feathers are full of things that capture her attention. In the midst of excavating her right wing, an urgent matter presents itself in her left and her head swivels to attend to it. Her movements are sharp and electric, whereas Gloria is bumbling and easily distracted. Darkness is leaner but capable of doubling in size without warning, as is any bird. The doubling is part of the grooming routine, separating the feathers and, I expect, allowing a chicken to see what she's after, though she just as often jabs blindly into her coat without fluffing and appears to be satisfied with the results either way. If the light is right, as a chicken fluffs its feathers, there is afforded a brief glimpse of the diminutive form inside. This is especially true of Darkness because her feathers are black, placing the pale flesh of her body in high relief. The body is compact, two small phones of meat in a basket of bone. The sight of this underlying truth—its smallness—is disarming, like a woman without hair.

Darkness lies on a flat stone, but she would never lay an egg there. Chickens do not lay eggs on rocks. A nest is a good idea and a rock is among the worst. While an egg can withstand incredible pressure delivered equally on all sides, it can withstand almost no force of the kind nature delivers: random vectors.

When the chickens are frightened, they seek cover between the house and the stairs, in the spirea. The bush is a white cloud of flowers each spring but otherwise a mess of branches, part nest, part cage. The chickens are not spooked by the ongoing trains, but on the occasion that a second train has just begun from the rail yard, one mile down the line, its beginning—the sheer chthonic force of it—stops the chickens in their tracks. Feet stuck, feathers still, every meaty muscle frozen, save for their hearts beating wildly and their roving eyes. In the same way, the train reaches into my sleep at night, its velocity morphed by dream into some great wall of water or bottomless pit.

THE HEAT DID NOT BREAK in the night. Yesterday reached 103 degrees as the chickens moved from one patch of shade to the next, digging fresh troughs in the shaded dirt. Chest-deep in the cool earth, they continued to pant, breasts heaving forward and back. More chickens die of exposure to heat than any other natural condition. I was surprised to learn this during our second year of owning chickens. The summer prior had been the hottest on record and it seemed a mere fluke that our flock of four had survived it. Hot weather has always been little more to me than an inconvenience, another means of dividing the people of the world into two parts: those who love heat and those who don't, though it often surprises me to find those who love it living among us in Minnesota, where they settle for five or so scorching days each year. These five or so days are the most dangerous to a chicken, contrary to every natural inclination toward sunlight.

Except for the hottest and coldest days of the year, I fill the outside feeder because the sun shines on it directly in the late morning. Chickens need as much sunlight as possible. They need the heat, which is trapped in their feathers as in a greenhouse. Thus the heat of the sun hovers around a chicken in an exact chicken shape. From the heat and the D vitamins and, of course, the pellets and the water, an egg is formed. First with a soft shell like the egg of an amphibious creature, the soft form better suited to tight quarters, then hardening into the brittle armor of an egg. Once an egg is formed, the light does not stop there. Light enters an egg from every side and leaves the egg likewise, though diminished, the egg having taken what it needs. An egg appears to glow because it glows.

I N THE SWELTERING morning Darkness and Gloria hammered back and forth. I am always comforted by chicken sounds first thing in the day for the obvious reason—they are alive. But beyond the first reassuring trumpet, I am compelled to silence them. If not for my own sake, for the sake of the neighbors, though it is for myself also in that the noise of a chicken is perfectly designed to agitate. There is no faster way to silence a chicken than to feed it.

I slipped on the green rubber boots kept just inside the back door. From the landing I could see that all was as I left it the night before, pophole open, shed door gaping wide. On the hottest nights of the year we leave the door to the shed open, along with the pophole to the outdoor run, to circulate air throughout the coop. But why had the chickens not yet emerged? Not even as a shaft of morning light swept the brown dirt clean. If the flu were to announce its arrival in some form, if the end were marked by a beginning—though, of course, the end has already begun—would this be the sign?

As the pellets pelted down into the outdoor feeder, the chickens cowered in the corner of the coop. When the dust had fallen, though it fell by first completing its rise, the chickens still did not acknowledge the bountiful feeder. This had never before happened. The chickens are not happy with the organic feed, but each day they approach the feeder matter-of-factly, having forgotten they are unhappy with the organic feed. Over the years I have often seen one chicken, deemed the lowest in the order by the rest of the pack, linger in the corner as a feeding frenzy ensued. This is not only common among chickens, it is natural. A beta chicken is most easily recognized by the cautious distance it maintains from the tin feeder. Gam Gam became the beta chicken before dying, but there is no reason to believe she died as a result of it. For a brief while she was fodder for attack by the others but shortly thereafter was treated only as an outcast. By the time of her death, Gam Gam so predictably occupied the corner of the coop during feeding time that a perfect cast of her underside marked the spot when she left the coop. And after she died, the hollow remained, for weeks on end, when I could not bring myself to sweep it clean.

FROM THE DOORWAY of the coop I searched the horizon, stopped short on all sides by the neighborhood. The rotting shutters of the house next door; the back of Rita's home, where the lowest of two steps has been chipped to pieces by the blade of a shovel; the crooked hoop in the back lot, beneath which a group of ragtag boys often gathers with or without a ball, but at this moment the boys were nowhere to be seen. There was no sign of danger.

Two nights before, Percy had heard a ruckus on the driveway. He left the house with a flashlight and returned a minute later. "You're not going to believe this," he said. It has been my experience that Percy is always overstating the matter, which is precisely why I followed him out the back door, to calibrate the experience for myself. I suppose there was also a part of me that wanted him to be right.

I followed him down the steps, along the sidewalk to the waist-high fence separating the yard from the drive-way and the alley beyond. There, in the dim glow of the streetlight, the largest raccoon I have ever seen was filling a suitcase with garbage from the overturned bin. The raccoon was unconcerned with our presence, could sense we were idiots or pacifists or, at the very least, unarmed. His sleek coat shifted from side to side over his broad back as he lifted each piece of garbage to determine what brought him joy. In the briefcase open beside him—Percy's own brief-case, discarded on account of opening with such ease—he placed four paper plates bearing remnants of cake, a length of gold ribbon shaved into curls, and the entire ball of lint and dirt purged from my bagless vacuum. When he had exhausted the contents of our bin, he closed the briefcase, stood on his two hind feet, and walked away as if to an all-important night shift elsewhere.

There had been no sign of his return the following morning and there was still no sign. From the open doorway of the coop, through the haze of dust, the chickens' combs seemed neither healthy nor different, more khaki than red.

BY LATE MORNING the chickens had not touched their food, nor could I find them. I ruffled the tops of the hostas and prodded the spirea with the handle of a broom. I knelt alongside the lowest step and peered beneath it to find a whole fleet of tiny maples sprouting from split seeds and, in their midst, an extra-large egg. I brought the egg into the light, where its pale blue shell seemed cut from the pale blue sky, a pure and perfect blue.

I held the egg aloft like a talisman. Both chickens rose up from a deep pit along the fence, flapping their wings to dispel the dirt. The grass shivered beneath them as in a sudden shower of rain. Then, as if time could be stretched by wonder, each thing had all the time it needed: the chickens still rising, the grass a-shiver, the supple light of midday lending the chickens and their combs a hearty healthy glow. Even the egg was boundless, lost in the blue sky above.

The chickens also were curious. I placed the egg on the ground between them. I had no idea what would happen. I thought perhaps the mother hen would claim it. I should not have been surprised when the chickens began to peck the candy-colored shell as if the whole thing were made of chocolate.

"WHAT'S THIS, a blue egg?" Percy said. I had set the fractured egg on the edge of the sink in a ridged slot meant to hold a sponge. Placed just so, the egg had authority, as if the sink had been made with this purpose in mind. "Where did it come from?"

"Under the stairs."

"Outside, you mean?"

Of course it was a blue egg and of course I did not find it in the house. These are the sounds of marriage: no question is meant to be answered. The important point about the egg—and this is a point of sheer logic, thus it escaped me—was that the egg could only have been laid by a bird that lays blue eggs. Because we do not have a bird that lays blue eggs, this point would have led me to a neat conclusion, namely, the blue egg had been laid by some other bird. While this thought had not occurred to me—I'd been thinking only of miracles—this was the point from which Percy began.

"What kind of bird would lay this?" Percy said. "Rita will know."

RITA'S BACK DOOR opened in advance of our arrival. She filled the doorway in her bibbed smock and slippers. "What a surprise," she said in an opposite manner. "Let me see." She took the egg in one hand and removed her glasses with the other. She placed the glasses on her head and reached for a second, more colorful pair, dangling in front of her on a bright cord thrust outward by her bosom.

"It's broken," she announced.

"The chickens broke it."

"You have a duck now?" she asked.

"That's it!" Percy said.

Percy reclaimed the egg and hurried through the alley to the backyard. He placed the egg in the shade beneath the stairs. The sun was high in the sky. The chickens scattered from Percy's path as he made straight for the coop, opened the door, turned on the light, and let out a whoop that sent both chickens running for the farthest corner of the yard.

"I knew it, she's here."

A plain brown duck emerged from the pophole. She was in no hurry, or all signs of hurry were masked by her webbed feet and her duck-tailed bottom swinging to and fro. She aimed her breasts over the piece of wood lining the open gateway to the yard and flopped down on the other side, then looked around with mild curiosity. Percy ran to the garage, clattered through his collection of objects, and appeared again with a plastic milk crate and a ragged towel. Meanwhile, the chickens had noted the size of the duck's bill and wanted nothing to do with her.

The duck reached the stairs, had smelled the egg or spotted a reminder or was drawn to the same spot by the same force that had drawn her there before. Percy waited alongside the stairs for a perfect poach. When she reappeared, unfazed by the broken egg—the egg in its brokenness bore no resemblance to the one she had left there—Percy placed the crate upside down on top of her, shimmied the towel beneath it, and flipped the whole thing over, leaving the duck trapped flat on her back. He gave the crate a jog to right her, whereupon the duck's feet slipped through the wide holes and she began to paddle. I set the blue egg beside her. As Percy marched toward Webber Pond, the poor duck swam out of sight.

The chickens returned to the coop at nightfall. They crossed through the pophole with great scuffle and squawk and stopped just inside, stock-still like sentries. They remember, I thought. They remember the duck.

I slept so soundly thinking this—the chickens

remember—and therefore believing that my time with the chickens had been equal in some measure to their time with me. They remember me. But, in the morning, down on my knees to scrape the floor of the coop, I saw what had stopped them in their tracks. Stuck in a brim of straw, a plain brown feather with a dash of blue.

I T IS JUNE and the trees are full of leaves, causing the shadows also to have leaves, and leaves of both kinds move in the wind, making a shadow of the wind. Darkness notes all of this and finds no threat, so she lies, not laying, calm yet alert. A red ant crawls from the stone where Darkness rests to a black feather of her tail, followed by a brown spider. The spider gains on the ant, though this does not appear to be the spider's goal; having come even with the ant, the spider forges on ahead with its two-leg advantage, toward the chicken's wing and onto it, while the ant doubles back to the tail. Darkness is unaware or she knows them to be what they are, neither harmful nor savory. She continues to groom around the ant and the spider, nosing each wing, then farther back. There is only one part of her body she cannot reach, beyond her tail. I suppose to see what happens there would be her undoing, chickens being so easily entertained.

Gloria is close at hand in the hostas, can be heard pecking the plants to pieces from the interior, and every so often

I spy the mottled fan of her tail. If chickens were not pack animals, they would still move about as such because they are interested in the same things. The comfort of the cool stones attracts them both and soon the two chickens groom next to each other, smoothing and shaping the fronds of their feathers in quick movements, entirely self-absorbed though the act appears coordinated, Darkness lying down and Gloria on her feet. The quiet clack of beak on quill is double time between them like a steady march of acrylic nails. It is soothing to watch them and it seems soothing to them also, the way they better the feather with each sweep of their beaks. There is such surety in their movements, as if this act of grooming, this solitary selfish act without hurry of any kind, is, in fact, their sole purpose here on earth. Then the beat of their work slows and softens until it stops altogether. First one, then the other, folds her feathered head beneath her wing, leaving only her comb visible, the lobed flesh from outer space an ordinary red.

A HEALTHY CHICKEN SHINES. Feathers belong to a family of natural luminescence. Included in this group spanning past, present, and future life are fish scales and butterfly wings and the skin of bright berries as the sun passes through them, the glowing eye of an animal when lit at night, the interior of the shell of an abalone, the intricate glitter of the flower of a violet. The leaf of a begonia shatters light when struck with sun, green as viewed from above or red as viewed from below; so do the leaves of a hosta appear to flicker at some point each cloudless day. While seated on the bus, I have seen the back of the neck of a young boy sparkle in this way, so perhaps we, too, are part of the family of glitter and light.

The chickens' feathers appear more lustrous now than ever before. Yes, sparkle and shine are signs of cleanliness, but what makes a feather shine is not purely superficial. The shine of a feather is an indication of good health, just as the original sparkle, the very reason we are drawn to all things sparkling—that of water on the horizon—was the promise of life itself. An object that ceases to shine is old or unwell and, either way, is closer to dying.

PERCY AND I made a list of the pros and cons of leaving our home here and moving west near the university. I never make lists, save for the lists in my head, whereas economists make a living by transcribing every thought they have onto paper, often in list form. For every pro, there is an equal and opposing con, and vice versa. In the end, an economist will publish his list and make the decision he wanted to make in the first place. Our list was no exception. Exchange this house full of charm and foibles for another of the same. Trade proximity to my mother for proximity to his. Leave old friends. Make new ones. Forget the puckish youngsters on their too-small bikes. Enter the domain of puckish youngsters elsewhere. The adventure. The reality. The bureaucracy of the institution. The perks of the bureaucracy. The inexorable completion of Percy's book (a version of this list appearing therein).

"What about regret?" I asked.

"Put it down," Percy said.

"Which side?"

"Both."

"Cost of living?"

"Prorated."

"I can't think of anything else."

"What do you want?" Percy asked.

I could not tell him what I want exactly. I want something that will not end in disappointment.

"I'm excited to spend my life with you," he said. "No matter what happens."

I CHOSE GLORIA because my mother would appreciate her name and because Gloria is a stoic chicken of regal bearing and, moreover, she lays the most eggs. My mother is at heart a practical woman.

The chickens could sense something amiss, perhaps noted the car with its back hatch open wide, plastic bin at the ready therein, lined with straw, pellets sprinkled on top, a dish of water half full in the corner. I opened the top flap of the outdoor run and stepped inside. Even with the chickens trapped as they were, to catch one is no easy task. I lunged forward, arms wide, eyes closed, into an uprising of wings and toenails and groped in the general direction of the commotion. On the next go, my outstretched hands filled with feathers. I pulled them close. It was Darkness, her birdy heart working fast against me. On second thought, my mother would not care whether the eggs were large and the name classy. I placed Darkness, skittering, into the plastic bin, whereupon she hopped into the water, upended the dish, scrabbled the straw and pellets into a stodgy stew, then set to work testing the plastic walls for signs of life or weakness.

I had called my mother to suggest a test run with the chickens.

"What do you think about the chickens?"

"I've tried not to," she had said.

"I could bring one over to stay the weekend.

"Mom?"

"Oh, fine. Bring a chicken."

Throughout the trip, Darkness was shunted to and fro in her own mess. By the time I reached my mother's house, the plastic bin was peppered with dung and straw and bloated pellets. In the midst of the squalor, Darkness slept, had been sleeping since we passed the black steer of Osseo thirty minutes before, the chicken's head turned at an incredible angle and tucked beneath her wing.

WHEN A CHICKEN ARRIVES at a new home, it is home. The things a chicken wants are the things a chicken needs. This is too simple of an arrangement for the human mind to grasp.

My mother carried Darkness into the house, through the kitchen, where a fleshy porridge pulsed on the stove, and to the backyard. My mother opened her arms, and Darkness paused, cocked her head to the side in a brilliant imitation of thinking, flew several yards—the longest flight I have seen from any of our chickens—then landed without a glitch on two feet and pulled a worm from the ground on contact like a bird of prey. My mother cheered.

"Her name is Darkness," I said.

"How sad, I'll have to change that."

"It doesn't matter, she doesn't answer to it."

"I'm not surprised."

THE PORRIDGE was for Darkness, the recipe taken from a book on the subject of turning a backyard into a life-sustaining farm. The author of the book had done so in the '70s and lived long enough to tell about it, though I doubt much longer. If he didn't starve of stubbornness, the world had disappointed him to death. The book sat open to the page for high-protein chicken meal.

"Where do you find this stuff?" I asked.

"At the federation co-op."

"Fish meal? Maize meal? Rye meal? Wheat meal? Ground seashells?"

"They have it all there, except the seashells. I used the old wind chime."

Of course she did.

"Have the chickens ever had poultry rot?" she asked.

"I don't think so."

"What about blackhead?"

"You mean Darkness?"

"No. I mean blackhead—the disease."

I had never heard of blackhead or the rots of chickens, nor had I considered cooking healthy meal to be flung to the grasses by the sloppy spoonful. I had thought the chickens would be a source of entertainment for my mother and almost no trouble. I wished now more than ever that Darkness would lay a deep brown egg before morning.

MY MOTHER ADHERES to a strict dinner hour but conceives of dinner loosely. The refrigerator is always almost bare, whereas the freezer overflows with a historic record of near-spoil. Between the two, an egg would come in handy. My mother pushed a piece of chicken out of sight behind a jar of cherry peppers that stood like a pillar of my childhood, unchanged right down to the foremost red pepper flanked by green on every side.

"We eat chicken," I said.

"That's not my idea of hospitality." She was thinking only of Darkness. Animals have always occupied the fast lane to my mother's heart and this is exactly what I wanted for the chickens.

Percy and I do eat chicken. The chickens of the system, whose lives bear almost no resemblance to life at all. It is horrible to think of eating chickens with such horrible lives, which is why we don't think much about it. If Percy had thought long about it, he'd have written a book. Percy loves dichotomy, and this one in particular—the subject of pet versus dinner and the corresponding overlap—is as rich as they come. If I thought much about it, I would stay as far from the shrink-wrapped breasts of modern chickens as possible. All thinking aside, chicken is the friendliest meat.

My mother found a block of downy cheese, a piece of gray meat, and, from the freezer, the last two buns in the world. Her garden had been eaten by rabbits, but near the shed a patch of dandelions thrived. She sent me down the driveway with a scissors to harvest the leaves. I chewed on a bitter green as I picked them. My tongue began to itch. I could not help but think I was slowly dying or, rather, that the slowness of my dying had abruptly picked up speed. Each cut of the leafy weed produced a milk-white drop that trembled without dropping.

In the kitchen the dandelions received no treatment at all. I rinsed them, patted them, and spoke a thought out loud about the lettuce I most preferred. The buns had been toasted, the cheese trimmed, and the meat resurrected with the life force of ketchup. I could think of nothing to say that did not directly refer to our humble meal. My mother relayed Darkness's every movement. The chicken scratched the ground, two, three, four times, pecked the earth twice, raised her beak to the sky, shook her body from head to toe, stretched her wings, pecked the earth once more, found a worm—hurrah—then raised her beak to the sky for the second time where something caught her eye and held it. "This is great," my mother said, and she must have meant the chicken show because the salad was full of grit.

"Did you know that chickens eat rocks?" I said.

"Of course they do, they have gizzards."

IN THE MORNING I slipped from the house to silence Darkness with the last nub of cheese. Her trumpeting pride had reached into my sleep and become the voice of Helen. The strangeness did not occur to me or, in my dream, strangeness was the truth of all things. I could understand every word of Helen's bugle and squawk. Oh, Helen, that's funny, I thought, as she crowed without end. I awoke and the crowing continued, albeit without humor of any kind.

There was a splash of pink in the gray sky. On the step, in her robe, sat my mother. She watched Darkness march back and forth in a solitary parade. Nearby, on the ground, in a whorl of young lilies, lay two brown eggs. I had hoped for an egg as I fell asleep, closed my eyes to the image of a perfect brown one. Please, Darkness. Please, I had thought. Any egg at all would be perfect.

Two eggs had the opposite effect. I felt terrible. The act had no precedent. Could it have been the fishy gruel?

I found the skillet stacked high in the same old cupboard, the butter soft as always on the topmost plate. When the cast iron steamed, I cracked the shell on the edge and watched the egg spill out from between my prying thumbs. There was nothing unusual about the egg. Its yolk was the color of marigolds, broken and blooming. Its white was firm. I fished out a shard of shell with one empty half.

"If you break the egg on the counter, that won't happen."

So I did, pointedly, aiming for destruction, and got instead an immaculate crack. Into the pan went another grade-A specimen, whole sun cradled in aspic. Two medium yet spectacular eggs. What a small wasted miracle when one egg would have done just fine.

AS WE ATE our eggs and toast, two feathers floated past the sliding glass door. Downy feathers joined together with a bit of whatever connects one feather to another. To see two feathers this way, moving as one, is strange and, upon further thought, terribly strange. Feathers do not grow in pairs, nor do they travel as such. No sooner had this thought occurred to me—the terrible strangeness—than a small bird dropped from the sky to the ground below.

Birds are forever flying with a solid smack into broad

plate glass only to rise again. This bird had not flown, had simply fallen, slow and silent, one foot from the sliding glass door. I watched the wind move the feathers this way and that. "Oh dear," my mother said. She slid the door open and made a nest of her hand. "Oh dear," she said again, and she cradled it to her. The thing was not a bird at all, but a clutch of gray down the size of a lemon. My mother set out to find her, ball of feathers in hand like a lodestone, and I followed one step behind.

When we found Darkness there was not much left, a crown of tail feathers and the foot with one toe missing.

My mother does not cry easily and she did not look as if she might; rather, she looked like there was quite suddenly nothing left to do. She took a seat on the step and I sat beside her.

The sun was high in the sky when my mother suggested we feed the goats. She had fetched a shoebox covered in dust and placed the remains of Darkness inside it. On our way to the shed, she set the box on the heap of compost and I got the sense she would return to it later, to bury the box or what lay inside. "Oh, come here," my mother said. "It's nobody's fault, you know." And she folded me in, her shirt soft beneath my fingers and her smell unchanged.

P ERCY SPENT the morning hours on the back landing, sitting vigil with his notebook. He did not speak a word about his purpose, which I took to be secretive. I might not have noticed Percy's silence, except that I had been waiting for him to say the wrong thing. Anything, so that I might blame him for saying it.

Late in the morning I joined him on the landing, from where the tracks of the train cannot be seen but the train itself can. I don't know what I hoped for. Perhaps some evidence that if we sat in the same place at the same time, we might see the same things. Here was Gloria, right in front of us. And who would have imagined that a drab gray sky would cast her feathers in such astonishing silver light? She moved about in silence and without hurry, had laid claim to her sovereignty, or was dumbstruck with grief. Meanwhile, Percy noted each car of the passing train in turn, his pace a bit frantic as the train picked up speed: BNSF, Hanjin (2), Cosco, BNSF, Procor, GATX. I could go on and on, as will the most boring book ever written.

Long before we lived here, the trains of this neighborhood were passenger trains. Now the people are gone, as are the grand adventures. The train continues with no beginning or end in sight, sometimes a blur of color at close range, every word bled and gone, and sometimes slow, so slow that the grass beside it seems to move backward as the train stands still. When the train moves slowly, I often mistake its rumble for thunder, but at a steady clip, the sound of the train is the angry clatter of work being done, the never-ending work of trading places.

A s I scrubbed the old oak floor with a mixture of oil soap and warm water, a thought presented itself or, rather, an idea occurred to me. I could discern its quality, a sort of barbed intensity, but not the message. And yet, the thing demanded my attention, as if the errors of my past were about to be revealed. The thought or the truth, whatever it was, existed for a flick of the mind and then was gone. What had provoked it? The dull citrus of the wood-safe soap? The circling of my arm over the weathered boards? The sponge itself, gasping air and water? My muscles coiled in readiness, but what exactly was I to do? There was simply not enough information. I returned to the patch of floor I had just cleaned, sponge dripping, hoping to catch the same feeling in the same place.

I arrived home from cleaning to find a hawk, still as a gargoyle, perched on the railing of the back landing. The only advantage the railing holds over the many towering trees is a clear view of the chicken-high door from where Gloria would emerge if not for the hawk as sentinel. The hawk watched me or, rather, watched the entire world with me in it. Beneath the hawk's ultraviolet stare I was nothing more than a radiant pulse, pinned to the walk alongside my bucket of cleaners. The chicken was somehow wise to the hawk, had felt the same watched feeling I could not shake, or heard the faint nagging trill of the hawk's tongue.

There has been no sign of a hawk before, but this hawk had an air of experience, watching the pophole with a willful patience not like faith at all. The thought of the hawk's rigorous waiting spurred me to action. I swung my bucket of bottles and cloths in a wide arc at my side and the hawk's response was both measured and instantaneous, unfurling great shafts of feather and bone. With two glorious pumps—each swift motion the triumph of grace over effort—the hawk rose up and away, to a far elm from where she resumed her watch of the world.

In the coop, Gloria occupied the far corner, striking the wall in one spot only and with diligence, as if each stroke brought her closer to the other side. She had no sense that freedom would be the end of her. What does it mean that a chicken's natural instincts are so counter to her well-being? I suppose only that what is natural is beside the point.

"Don't worry," I said. "The hawk is gone."

G LORIA WOULD LIVE her whole life in the garden, if undeterred. She has not learned how to enter the garden despite entering the garden often and always by the same route, through the large gaps in the fencing versus the numerous smaller gaps on either side. The length of fence was left behind by the previous owners of the house, who must have used it for decoration only, though the fence is not so decorative as this suggests: prefab and low-lying, made of heavy wire dipped in a thin coat of flexible green plastic and hinged at three-foot intervals to conform loosely to shape or whim. Common garden thieves traverse the fence with ease, such as the vast supply of chubby rabbits in the neighborhood that by some good fortune prefer the neighbors' lettuces to our own, a fortune measured only in lettuce, this year a bit yellow with brown spots.

Until the chicken's most recent incarnation—a bird made desirable by the margin its breasts outweigh the rest of its body—chickens flew from place to place. Early chickens were adept at flying. An adept flying chicken would have soared down from the sweeping sky to coast just above the ground until the weightlessness of adept flying transferred directly into the awkward loping gait that probably has not changed much since the dawn of chickens. Perhaps somewhere there is a length of petrified mud attesting to all of this.

Gloria sticks her head into the small gaps in the fencing, through which only her head will fit, pushes her head in as far as possible, until her breasts press up against the sturdy wire. At this point she is, for all practical purposes, trapped. Chickens do not move backward. A chicken moves only into space that can be seen. Every third time or so, the exact number complicated by randomness, Gloria approaches a larger gap in the fencing and gains entry to the garden beyond.

Upon entering the garden a chicken first eats the kale. I have no idea why a chicken who prefers scratch grains to all else makes an exception of kale. Perhaps the punch of a chicken's beak through the sturdy leaf of the green is a merry diversion of its own. After the kale has been stripped bare, a chicken rakes in the black dirt until she has subdued her appetite with crisp-backed roly-polies, common worms, and the occasional grub, plump as a pool toy. Thus satisfied, a chicken rakes a pit of earth the width of her body and descends thereinto, her chesty upper half breaching the surface like the figurehead of a vessel moored belowground.

The behaviors of a chicken have not changed much over time. Precursors of all domestic animals had sharper teeth and sharper claws and ate each other, their own kind not excepted, far more casually than the animals of today. But chickens still have sharp claws and, despite having no teeth, they are still carnivorous animals, eating baby birds and mice that happen across their paths with a casual disregard like snacking, and often resort to bullying one of their own in a ferocious manner that may or may not lead to the death of the bullied chicken. Compared to cats and dogs and even the most impressionable breeds of pigs, chickens seem barbaric, but the modern chicken is perfectly suited to the life it leads.

H ELEN'S HOUSE is lovely to look at and terrible to live in and perhaps a reasonable investment if the owner is keen on the value of experiences. It was built, foremost, as a concept—spirals in on itself like a snail—though the architect himself lived in the house for several years until he tired of its specific charms. Helen once earned commission on the sale of the house. On the second go-round she could resist neither its charms nor its lack of resale value. I am familiar with every inch of the Fibonacci House because I have cleaned it top to bottom on both occasions. The first marked my return to cleaning after many years away from it. I had stopped cleaning houses to become a mother, but then what? It turns out the world accepts failure only insofar as you keep trying. I had not prepared myself for what I might do next. It was Helen who suggested I clean again, then she hired me to do it.

Helen invited us for dinner. She has never before done so but has always imagined it, told us this as she led Percy on a tour to the center of the house, that her image of us din-

ing at her table was some small part of the reason she had
bought the house in the first place. (Helen makes a point
of not cooking and does not entertain, so it is hard to say
what this imagining entailed.) The center of the house is
a drastic curve that can never be inhabited, merely groped
into with a curled hand or an expensive attachment for
cleaning such things. Helen explains the interior as going
on and on forever, though I have only ever experienced it
differently: as a place where things get stuck. For this reason, the inner curve of the house serves as Johnson's play-
room. A length of toddler fencing spans the curve ten feet
out and his toys litter the dwindling space. Helen bought
the house before Johnson could crawl and, throughout the
year since, has been too fearful of the spiral staircase to
allow him upstairs. Johnson's crib occupies the kitchen, not
far from the stove. To have slept in the kitchen as a child
will be part of the boy's experience, and perhaps a notable
part, if he has any leaning toward food or away from it.

Toys cried out in their musical voices as Helen nudged
them aside with her bare feet. The closeness of the walls
charged the air around us. In the bended light, Helen
looked pregnant. She does not have the type of body that
often appears this way, though the effect of the house was
incalculable. I hid my surprise by joining Johnson on the
floor, where he tended to his work in an important manner,
tapping his toys in turn with a plastic hammer. He gave

me a serious look—perhaps wise to my particular emotional state wherein crying could go either way—then set down his hammer and scavenged about until he found a limp rabbit with one arm, which he brought to me and held against my face.

As Helen returned from the abyss, her dress clung to the walls in front and back and her hair had come to life. Then, upon reaching some critical distance, the silk shrank against her body and her hair fell limp on her shoulders and she was just Helen, not full of magic like moments before. "Johnson," she said. "Don't put Bunny in faces. Bunny smells."

In the spacious outer curve, Helen demonstrated the original electronics of the skylight. The remote hummed and the rooftop window opened with a clunk. "When the wind blows over the open skylight, it sounds like the ocean," Helen said. She gave Johnson the remote. He squealed with glee and pressed both buttons until the hum of the remote changed to the sharp *zap zap zap* of a contraption used for killing flies. If the wind blew, we did not hear it. Meanwhile, Helen emptied the contents of two bags of salad and a plastic tray of shrimp into a broad bowl, red sauce and all. When the remote was secured from Johnson, in exchange for two cookies, the skylight refused to close. The meal consisted only of salad and a dish of pistachios pinched shut like mollusks, perhaps a decorative touch, though Helen twice cleared a nut, shell and all, from Johnson's mouth with the hook of her finger, then proceeded to crack it and eat it herself. This is the type of thing I will never know about myself, if I am the kind of person to eat that nut and, also, if I could be so watchful and dextrous and completely unfazed.

Helen refused my help with the dishes because the sink had not been fixed. A hole had been cut in the bottom of a plastic bucket and the bucket placed over the faucet to direct the spray. With Johnson asleep beside it, the stakes were too high or the outcome too predictable, by which I mean the experience.

A HOUSE FALLS APART. This is never more apparent than when a house must be sold, but it is not more true at this point than any other. I have charted the growth of a crack in the kitchen ceiling for the six years I have lived in this house, first mistaking it for a cobweb when it measured not half the length of the duster in my hand. Since then it has stretched across the pebbled surface, leaving a fine dust on the floor below. Now the whole of it measures the length of a broom handle. Percy does not believe me, though my slapdash measurements suit his style. Percy believes only what he hopes to be true. He predicts the next generation will return to their roots, via chickens, among other things, though he has amassed no evidence in support of this. He cites instead all evidence to the contrary as proof of a breaking point, fixed in the future. Whereas my worries and my theories are often indistinguishable from each other, which I suppose makes me a fatalist, except that I would like to be wrong.

Meanwhile, a hairline crack has appeared on the ceil-

ing of the living room. There is also a fault in the drywall along the stairs leading into the basement. I can rest a
nickel on the ledge where the drywall has shifted out from
the wall above. Two years ago, the ledge would not hold
a dime. A house on the market sits and sinks, and yet, it
must somehow suggest a better life is possible, right here
and now. In our neighborhood this is not the most obvious
conclusion, nor is it helped along by the onslaught of backyard fireworks beginning a week in advance of the Fourth
of July and continuing still, a week past, as often as not
before dark.

THE TORNADO left a manic path of destruction from where
it first touched down at the intersection of Penn and Lowry
in the seedy center of North, to the edge of the Missis-
sippi two miles northeast. All along its route lie crumbling
houses and slouching porches and fences that are surely
failing to do whatever they were put there for. Orange
notes of foreclosure hang willy-nilly on front-door windows like the christening of a brand-new holiday. It is
impossible to say if the tornado is responsible for any of
this, or how much, and for which of the many dying trees.

P ERCY GLEANED exactly one insight from our dinner with Helen—she is the person to sell our house—whereas I had assumed it all along.

"Of course I'll sell it," Helen said, "but I won't be happy about it."

Helen came to inspect the house. I had thought she would bring Johnson, even though to do so would be unprofessional. I was surprised to see her alone and was surprised also by my disappointment. I suppose I'd been hoping the whole house-selling thing could be as unprofessional as possible.

She wore a boxy blazer cuffed at the wrist, professional attire, but useful also for masking her stomach entirely from view. I assumed she had chosen the blazer for that very reason. Why, though she did not look pregnant—had looked pregnant for only one time-bent moment—could I not stop thinking that she was? But, of course, she couldn't be. Helen would never wait to tell me until I could see for myself.

We toured the house together, Helen calling out the bright spots as they occurred to her: good bones, hardwood, new windows, gas stove, the chickens. She watched Gloria from the kitchen window. The chicken stood on a stone in a beam of sunlight, looking magnificent.

"What about the chickens?" Helen said.

"It's just Gloria now. My mother's taking her."

"Not soon, I hope. A chicken could make all the difference in your neighborhood."

"They'll need to get their own permit," I said.

"I meant the idea of a chicken. A concept chicken."

"She's not that smart."

Helen laughed and then laughed harder and then began to cry. "I'm sorry," Helen said. "I'm just—I'm going to miss your funny little farm."

"Does the maple look sick to you?" I asked.

"It's lovely. I love its drape."

"That's what I'm worried about."

"The tree is fine."

"It's falling apart."

"Oh, please, don't," Helen said, and she turned to the alley as if intent on the passing train.

I LET MYSELF into the Villa on Queen. Something was off in the house, I could tell right away. The interior had recently been painted; the paint smelled wet though it was dry, but the smell alone did not account for the feeling. I began to clean the bathroom as I always do: sink, tub, toilet, floor, mirror last of all. Every surface was already clean. It was as if the house had been cleaned before my arrival and been cleaned to a standard higher than my own.

I continued on with the motions of cleaning—there was no obvious way to confirm the cleanliness of the house but to clean it again. As I mimed my usual act, I felt the futility of each task. The work was stripped of all sense of reward, and it occurred to me I was experiencing cleaning in the way the average person might. Weren't things clean enough already? And if we can't agree on that, what's the point? The feeling worsened with each room of the house and did not subside as I poured the final bucket of water, still limned with soap, into the sink and rinsed my cloth to wipe the baseboard on my way out the door.

I drove home, uneasy, with the radio loud to prevent thinking, but I could not drown out the words of Helen from long ago, which have come to mind many times since: "From my experience, you might be trying too hard." She had meant it kindly or perhaps to be funny, and, of course, she could not foresee what the future held, for me or for her, and, either way, she was probably right.

I THINK I would have been a good mother, especially the older I get. Perhaps this is why the idea of being a mother is difficult to let go of. I care less now what others think and who likes me and how I look—all variations, of course, on the same thing. Though it continues to pain me when I consider that others might see me as someone who never wanted children. They must see me this way. I feel I understand people who don't want children—they are tired or there is an episode of their childhoods they cannot bear to repeat or their lives lack that punishing sense of incompleteness—but I don't want to be mistaken for them. Even as I am often tired and my childhood was not a perfect model and I would gladly shed the notion of a life less than whole. Maybe I would have been a terrible mother. It stands to reason that I do not have the knowledge or the experience or a resounding vote of confidence coming from any particular direction. I have only the idea that I might have been good. The lasting idea.

A CHICKEN RACKET roused me in the night. Gloria was awake and provoked—a chicken does not wake in the night any other way. I sprang from the bed and reached the coop in one fluid sequence, as if I had trained my whole REM-sleep life for this moment. My swiftness left me thoroughly unprepared. There, locked in the outdoor run, though it had somehow gained entry, a raccoon the size of a small child clung to the wire with four shrill paws. The pins and needles of its teeth flashed beneath the streetlight as Gloria cringed in the corner. She had dug a small trench there, for what seemed the sole purpose of burying her head. From this vantage she could not see that I had come to save her.

I flung the gate open and through the mesh of the fence delivered a swift kick to the animal's silver stomach, whereupon it snarled in warning. Its hands gripped the wire so fiercely, as if its hands were also made from wire, the same wire, and had found in this fence their perfect counterpart; were twisted and locked in place until some greater meal presented itself on the other side. I pried the fingers of the front paws loose as I centered another kick, and the animal landed belly up with a sick thud. I would not have thought to grab the rake but there it was, in my hand; nor would I have thought to stick the butt end through the wire to protect the chicken, but that is what I did. I was not one bit afraid, or my fear was unrecognizable as such, pulsing like a thing outside me in the warm dark night. The air sparked with possibility. What would I do next? I rather hoped it would involve a feat of superhuman strength. I guarded Gloria from above as the raccoon slunk low-bodied over the board that serves as threshold and stopped just out of reach. I turned to the animal to watch it watch me. If I had not moved, we might have stayed that way till morning, eyes locked in the dark, but I swung the rake to and fro, and growled so deep and loud I began to cough. It was the cough that scared the animal away, over the fence and to the parkway, where a slow-moving car stopped altogether to let it pass.

FEATHERS CIRCLED the run of the coop, but Gloria, eyes closed to the world, appeared unmarred. I crawled into the low-lying doorway to reach her and pulled her to my chest. A shower of gray petals fluttered to the ground around my feet. "You're safe now," I told her, though my voice shook.

I hoped my pounding heart would calm her as hers comforted me: she was alive.

Percy appeared then, holding a rolling pin bigger than his arm, ready to, who knows what? Roll out a ball of dough? But he was there, nonetheless. He said my scream had woken him. He had heard a woman's scream and thought it was the type of wild cat that screams like a woman. I don't know why he heard a woman and thought of a cat, but neither one of us could quite believe I had done it, even as my blood raced wildly and my feet seemed to hover some distance off the ground. Percy searched every inch of the coop for a point of entry as I looked on with Gloria in my arms. He found no hole or tear, no earth upturned, no silver hairs caught in the clenched wire. There was no evidence of the assailant. Percy did not say a word, but perhaps we arrived at the same conclusion. If the hole could not be found, it could not be fixed. Or, if there was no hole, I had locked the animal in the coop myself. But this was impossible. The animal had been there, quite impossibly, and in the same way, it might return.

I stroked the slender feathers of the chicken's neck. She made a sound like purring that I have always thought suggested contentment. Her eye against me was neither open nor closed. In a flash of horror I saw the socket had been scooped clean. Her gleaming eye was gone and, in its place, a slick black void.

GLORIA has always been a beautiful heather-gray chicken, but now her beauty is that of a fairy tale: the beautiful chicken with one monstrous eye. If she was not the last of our chickens, the deformity might have accrued some benefit of character, but she is alone.

Gloria stands always with her missing eye to the wall. She sees only with her right eye and, because the right eye of a chicken is the nearsighted eye, she sees only what is right in front of her. With her left eye gone, Gloria cannot see anything beyond a few feet: not the red fox passing on the parkway, not the hawk high on the nearest pole, not the bald eagle sighted one block from our house, where it touched down just long enough to feast on the entrails of a discarded White Castle hamburger. It seems to me the chicken's blindness will make no difference in the narrow confines of her life with us. We will protect her or we will not.

. . .

I WAKE more and more in the night, willing my breath to silence, not knowing if it was a dream or the world that woke me. I slip out of bed and down the stairs and outside to check on the chicken. The glow of the moon or the nearest streetlight is most often not enough to mark her shape on the perch through the small window of the coop. I carry a flashlight to shine on her, and because I do not want to wake her with the beam of light, I shine it through my cupped hand and hold my hand to the window. It is eerie to behold my glowing fist and its reflection in the window and, in its dull red glow, the chicken sleeping there. If Gloria was to wake at that moment, my hand would be the morning sun. In the dead of night, her world revolves around me. I'm sure of it then, as she sleeps, but in the light of day it seems unimportant. If Percy knows I leave the bed and return some time later he has never mentioned it. He always seems to be sleeping soundly upon my return.

PERCY HAS NO TROUBLE SLEEPING. His secret, because I've asked, is that he doesn't see the point of lying in bed awake. Good for him and his all-encompassing reason. When I lie awake, I sometimes think of his ex-girlfriend, who no doubt lay awake beside him on the same side of the bed I sleep on now, and perhaps even asked of his secret for sleeping, then thought as she lay awake, good for him. I have never met this woman, but I have seen her picture. A handful of such pictures exist in overlooked places around the house. I have searched high and low for more but discover them only by mistake, the pictures hard to find for the same reason they exist at all: they have been forgotten. Her wild cloud of dark hair suggests a sort of rampant fertility. When I find these pictures, I feel strange and small, if only because I am different from another thing he loved.

THE GREEN LEAVES have fallen willy-nilly around the yard all summer long and, though I have never known the maple to lose green leaves, it does not surprise me. As I filled my bucket with leaves, one by one, Cal's massive vehicle trundled into the back alley. He pulled past his old driveway, then backed into the space, then forward, then back, then forward again, then the fading metallic click of something wrong with the motor that was probably not worth fixing. He stepped from the vehicle and jockeyed with the latch of the door before looking up.

"Saw the sign out front," he said. "Thought we better stop, seeing as it might be the last time."

He was right, I supposed. In all likelihood this would be the last time. It seemed a bit unfair to show up unannounced and then announce something better left unsaid. On top of that, Percy had set off on an errand minutes before.

"I was just tending the garden," I said.

"Lynn's grandma's expecting us." He turned to the wagon.

We watched Katherine climb over the back seat to the front, headfirst. The horn beeped, the visors went down and up, Lynn's hair moved about with purpose.

Katherine emerged from the front of the vehicle, her lips painted a garish red. It seemed for a moment the world had sped on without me. Here was Katherine, looking grown up or, at the very least, trying the look, her lipstick applied in a haphazard manner, so that up close the fine hairs of her upper lip could be seen beneath it, also painted red.

Lynn stepped close and said, "Katherine thought the chickens would like her better if she wore lipstick." Lynn's smile suggested I, too, might be delighted by Katherine's thinking. All mothers do this, of course, share the quirks of their children as tender asides, quite certain it will be the highlight of everyone's day. But only a mother can turn these shining snapshots of her children into joy. To share them benefits no one. Any other mother feels outdone, and anyone who isn't a mother feels something else, some impossible distance from the privacy of motherhood. And perhaps Katherine was right about the lipstick: Gloria did not pay her any mind, whereas the chicken had always before run away from her.

"Katy can do a chore, clean the coop or what have you," Cal said. "We'll all pitch in."

The coop has never been so clean as it is now. We hope to suggest the space could be used for anything. It had

206 / Jackie Polzin

once been a garden shed and with very little effort it might be again. Cal disappeared into the coop, followed by the clutching scrape of the metal dustpan on the concrete floor.

"I always wanted a yard like yours," Lynn said. She looked across the alley at her old garden, where the weeds towered above the unmown grass, then back to the bucket in my hand. "I guess I didn't have time."

Gloria pecked the remains of the hostas that bordered the fence and froze in the shadow of a passing cloud. Katherine did not miss her chance and Gloria did not resist. Against the girl's small chest Gloria seemed giant but also strangely calm, even as Katherine buried her face in the stiff silver feathers of the chicken's wings.

"What happened to your eye?" Katherine said, as if Gloria might answer. The socket had hardened into a thick shell as black as burned wood. I might have picked the whole thing off if I had the nerve to see what lay beneath it.

"A raccoon got her," I said.

"Does it hurt?"

"It's just a scab."

"Why is she crying? Is she sad?"

Gloria was not crying; rather, the crust of her blackened eye had a sort of sheen to it. Chickens don't cry. There is no convincing argument for why a chicken does not cry— they're equipped to cry—except that a crying chicken cannot see so very well. It stands to reason that Gloria could afford to cry now, would be compromising nothing in doing so.

"She's lonely," I said. "Chickens don't like to be alone."

"But I'm right here," Katherine said. She hoisted Gloria onto her shoulder to balance the heft. From a certain angle the bird was a glamorous scarf and Katherine the eccentric ingénue.

"Chickens need other chickens," I said.

"Where are they?"

Cal's voice rang out. "Remember what I said in the car, Katy? About chicken heaven?"

Whatever Cal had said in the car, he had not been specific enough. In the years they lived across the alley, I had often referred to our backyard this way, which seemed to be the source of Katherine's confusion. She walked the edge of the fence and each row of the garden. She picked apart the hostas with the toe of her purple shoe and circled the maple, stopping once to peer back swiftly as if a chicken might be following her, perhaps on account of the lipstick. When every other space had been scrutinized, Katherine squatted to peer beneath the low deck. Gloria jumped to the ground, ran the length of the yard and straight into the coop. "They're not here," said Katherine.

"Oh, honey," Lynn said. "The chickens are way up in the sky now."

I CAUGHT GLORIA with ease, pinned always to the wall as she is now. Percy had filled a box with straw, then thought it a bit too crude and tucked a towel over the straw so the whole resembled a crib from the pioneer days. My mother was expecting us and, furthermore, expecting us to leave Gloria in her care. No sooner had the trip to my mother's been planned than I knew I could not do it. I called twice to break the news, but each time my mother had news of her own. First, the neighbor would build her a coop. And then, two days later, my resolve hastened by the pending coop, the neighbor had already done it, was the kind of person who stood by his word as quickly as possible. If I called again she would be cooking porridge for chickens and, what's worse, she would know I had called three times to tell her. I had no choice but to deliver the news in person.

But no. I could not bear to tell her in person. Halfway to my mother's house, with Percy by my side, I stopped in a small town where I have only ever stopped to buy pie. I bought a pie and then had no excuses left. I called her from the sidewalk so that Percy would not hear me. He did not know I had not yet told her unless he knows me as well as he claims, a bit better than I know myself. In which case he would understand the pie for what it was and ask no questions when it spent the duration of our trip in its box on the floor of the car. I could not give her a pie instead of a chicken.

My mother did not answer the phone. I was not prepared to tell her as I did, without pause into the steel trap of a machine. I imagined it was the machine itself I was talking to and was thus able to say, quite matter-of-factly, we would not be leaving Gloria, she had lost an eye and we had brought the chicken with us only to keep her safe.

My mother greeted us on the driveway wearing a dress I used to love on her. I suppose it was a gesture of hospitality, the dress, though Percy would think nothing of it and I could think only of how frumpy the dress looked now, faded and frayed, and how my mother had failed to notice, had probably taken it from her closet with the same old fondness. She ushered us to the sunny side of the house where a shanty had been built in extension, crafted with the same siding and trim as the house itself, with a small slanted door. Next to the door was a slanted window, and through the window, a perch cut from the branch of a tree.

"The neighbor boy helped me build it," she said. "I

promised him eggs." This was not the work of a boy, so I was not surprised to learn the neighbor was someone I had known, a boy then, one year behind me in school. I knew also that she had not listened to the message. My mother has always insisted on telling the truth, as if the truth were something real and obvious. But surely it was not true that the chicken would only be safe with me, though this is what I felt, even as I held the bird's empty eye against me.

"Oh, let's try it out!" my mother said, swinging the door open.

I lifted Gloria to the perch. She stepped to it readily and shuffled toward the end, both feet knowing exactly what to do, each toe curling and uncurling in accordance with a particular sequence until the chicken reached the wall, which she must have felt with the tip of her wing because she could not see it. My mother clapped her hands in delight.

INSIDE THE HOUSE, the machine blinked. My mother listened to my voice as I stood beside her. Surely that's not what I sound like, I thought, my voice high and harsh and unyielding. There was no outward sign of the treachery of the message. When the talking had stopped, my mother smoothed her skirt. "All right, then," she said. "I hope you're hungry. There's a roast in the oven."

· · ·

THE COOP lay directly below my childhood window. I could see nothing but the tin roof, pink with the rising sun.

My mother was awake. How many times had she greeted me this way, from her seat at the table with a cup in her hands?

"Gloria is fine," she said. "I was just out to see her, though I suppose you'll want to see for yourself."

My mother was right, of course. Gloria was fine. Through the slanted window I noted the perfect balance of her sleep, head square on her chest with her eye closed softly. She could not have looked more at peace, brushed in the rose gold of morning, her feathers smooth against her body in the exact shape I think of as her.

The sound of the car's engine woke Gloria with a start. Percy always does this, wakes early at my mother's with an urge, I think, to escape. He cannot bear what he only suspects to be true, that returning to my mother's house has nothing to do with him. He backed down the drive to where it meets the county road, then drove off away from town.

MY MOTHER had poured me a cup of coffee. "Percy said he had work to do. I hope he knows he can do it here."

"It's probably research," I said. Though Percy had not told me, I knew what he had left to do. He would bring back a chicken. This was just the kind of work he preferred—to be the hero of an ordinary day.

There was something more my mother wanted to say, I could tell, as she stood from the table and moved to the fridge to inspect the contents. She is never otherwise one to hold the door of the fridge wide open. She hummed a quiet note, as if in preparation for a more important sound. Out came the roast spotted in firm white fat, a bundle of sprouting carrots, a stalk of limp celery, half of an onion in a bag for bread. Then she set about making soup from last night's dinner.

PERCY RETURNED with eight dozen eggs. A hen's yearly output, by his calculations, though it's unclear how he arrived at such an even number. It seemed to me both baseless and too high. Three flats of eggs that held three dozen each. How cheap it all seemed with the topmost flat part empty. How I wished for Percy to walk backward with the whole of it, back to the car, back down the road, back to the sagging barn or tarp-covered crates to return the lot.

"They're for the neighbor," Percy said. "The eggs you promised him."

My mother thanked him and set the eggs on the counter and began to rearrange the fridge.

THE GOATS were fed and the small hole they are always scratching was filled with dirt and in the dirt was a fat worm, which my mother brought to Gloria and I followed along, Percy having disappeared into the house somewhere, surrounded by dusty books. The soup sat all day on the stove and for dinner was served too hot. On top of the broth, the orange fat floated in pools so that each spoonful was a burning balm. Before my mother had finished, she laid her spoon on the table and put her hands in her lap. "When you were a girl, you refused to eat leftovers," she said. "Now look at you. I never imagined you'd have chickens." She picked up her spoon and continued to eat. She had said nothing, really, but I knew what she meant. I had her blessing with the chicken.

For breakfast there were eggs on toast and yellow muffins and, in the center of the table, a bowl of boiled eggs, still warm in their shells. Whatever Percy thought of this, he didn't say. Not then and not later, throughout the long drive home with Gloria silent in her box behind us, and the pie on the floor, untouched.

THE SIGN in the yard says HOUSE FOR SALE. A square of sod sits at the base of the sign, torn free from the grass around it. When the sign is finally taken away, sometime after we've gone, the sod will be placed back from whence it came. That is, unless the clod of dirt and grass is kicked to some other street entirely. I have twice recovered it, quite far down the road.

FROM THE MOMENT I saw Helen in her shapeless smock, I knew what she had come to say. It didn't matter why she had come, I was glad to see her.

She placed her hands on her stomach. "You were probably wondering," she said. "I didn't want to tell you until—" but she did not finish. She went on to say she had wanted a girl, not because she wanted what was best for Johnson, though obviously she wanted what was best for Johnson, but in this case she had wanted what she wanted despite that, until the baby was declared a girl, at which point she realized a girl would be best for Johnson, too.

Of course Helen would think this. Has always believed that what happens is best because her life has been good enough. I was not happy for her, strictly speaking, nor was I opposed to her happiness. Her baby girl was nothing more to me than another part of Helen I would miss.

"Hurray," I said.

I found tea and crackers, both stale, and Helen touched neither. She placed her feet on the chair beside her and spoke in the soft sounds of someone close to sleep. If I had not offered her the couch to lie on, she might have slept in the chair. Even so, I was surprised and a bit embarrassed, though I could not say who for, when Helen moved to the couch without hesitation, as if sleep was the only thing she could move swiftly toward.

"I'm sorry," she said. "I'm just so tired." And then she slept.

For three months of my life, I, too, slept in this die-hard fashion whereby sleep belonged to a set of the gravest responsibilities. It was completely new to me to sleep with such conviction, and proof that every action from this point forward would be new to me in some profound way. What a comfort to sleep like this, safe in the thought that life will go on acquiring meaning, even as you sleep.

G LORIA IS MISSING. She went missing in the afternoon, not in the night as I might have expected. At midday she was there in no unusual form and one hour later she was gone. In the meantime I heard nothing out of the ordinary, unless, and on this point I can't be certain, I heard nothing at all.

No chicken of ours has ever escaped, but I have always thought it would not be difficult to do, the act requiring neither intelligence nor foresight. A hop onto an upturned flowerpot or the railing of the stairs, followed by an up-down of the wings. I once watched Gam Gam jump to the top of the chicken run, three feet off the ground, and to the top of the high fence skirting the hostas. She stood on the narrow edge of the plank to which all the vertical posts are nailed and peered over the top of the peaked posts into the alley below. I did not dare move from where I crouched in the garden, trowel in hand. Several times Gam Gam opened her wings to traverse the slight rise and pawed the pointed board before her with her pronged toes.

She practiced the movements on her perch the same way I have seen a young woman—a dancer, I gathered, from her tight knot of hair—simulate an entire routine, rehearsing each move in miniature as she stood in the aisle of a city bus holding nothing at all. Wings open then closed, foot up then back. The air around Gam Gam shuddered with possibility. One step up and over and her life would never be the same. It seemed quite a matter of chance that instead she turned toward where I squatted, breathless amid the kale, and jumped down to the top of the chicken run from whence she came. Having reached the ground, she let out a tremendous squawk, then ran in frenzied circles as if to outpace the vision of what lay beyond.

P ERCY RETURNED from the garage with a can in each hand, taken from his pile of dearest junk and filled to half with scratch. I had been afraid for Gloria but my fear had not been real, was something of my own construction, until Percy stopped his work to join me. He thought I would not find her on my own or that I should not be alone when I did.

There are no bushes on the parkway in which a chicken might hide, only tall trees in sturdy rows with an odd sapling swapped here and there for the fallen. We rattled our rusty cans, and I did not allow myself to dwell on the fact that our only hope could be thus contained. I felt a fleeting oneness with the neighbors as the clamor of our search reached into their open windows. First to the statue with its circle of pines, then back past the house to Webber Pond. Surely it did not matter that our house was of similar construction to so many around us. Gloria knew nothing of the house, save for the back door and landing, and, either way, she could not see it. If she found water, it would be by chance. If she saw a fox, it would be upon her.

All around us wire-legged signs boasted the great team cheer of Camden: WE WATCH, WE CALL. I had never before found comfort in them. Upon returning home, Percy sent an urgent message to the group email chain: "Our chicken is missing, gray with spots. If you see anything [and this proved a point of confusion to the group at large], please reply."

IN THE MORNING the bed was empty beside me. Percy had been up late into the night sifting the myriad responses for any piece of news: one neighbor's cat had not seemed hungry, which she claimed was rare.

I spotted Percy from the upstairs window. He had likely been to the pond and was on his way back, hands clasped in front as when lost in thought. I had the idea of making coffee so that the smell would greet him when he opened the door, but I waited until it was too late and instead I stood and watched him. Upon reaching the shadow of the house, he looked up. He waved then, unsmiling, and in his other hand, the hand not moving, he held a feather. A single feather did not mean nothing, but it did not mean the worst.

. . .

PERCY SET THE FEATHER in my hand and the downy edges quivered. From its shape and size, it had come from her body, not her wing.

"Do you think it's her?" he asked.

"It's just one feather."

He placed his hand behind his head. "There were quite a few."

I left the house and walked around it to the exterior of the high fence, one foot from where I had seen her last. Here, on the outside, nothing had changed. A dog barked, a siren wailed, a lawnmower rumbled to life and began to cut, the buzz of its blade pulsing through the chickens' silence. I held the feather by the stem, smoothing the soft strands as if there were some wisdom to be coaxed from it. How had she flown or, if she had not, and I could not really believe she had, what had taken her? And what happened next? More than this, why did I want to know? I could not even bring myself to ask where he had found her, though he had knelt beside her and chosen this feather from among the rest.

IT IS EASY to leave an empty house. Percy and I have signed our names sixty-two times toward the selling. He has written this fact in his notebook, underscored with a straight bold line, whereas the words themselves are written in his trademark tremulous hand.

The woman who bought our house will not be disappointed. We know nothing about her except that she grew up down the street, where her mother still lives. The woman wanted only the location of this house, to be close to her mother but, presumably, not within view. She suffers no illusions regarding the neighborhood. I would like to think she got much more than her bid for location, but perhaps she cares not at all for the rest: the paint jobs, the curtains, the modern windows that flip inward to be washed with ease, not to mention the garden—ho-hum as it is—and the leafless yard and the stoic maple and the poppies planted upon Helen's suggestion that have now run their course, rising from the soil like spent bottle rockets. Someday, perhaps distant, perhaps not, the woman's mother will pass away, and even this will not change the value of our house to her; she will have done what she came to do.

I RETURNED from the parkway to the smell of bleach. This is not the way I would have done it but now it was done. Percy met me in the alley and walked with me to the house, and I could not help but think he had positioned himself alongside me to hide his work, the shed scraped and scrubbed to the point of newness and bleached to the point of who knows what? The smell of the chickens is gone—I suppose somewhere along the way I had grown fond of it—and gone with it is the sense that the chickens were ever here, save for a patch of bare earth marking the outdoor run, strewn with fine seeds of grass.

Acknowledgments

I would like to thank:

Lee Boudreaux, for her warmth and vision

Kishani Widyaratna, for caring boldly

The whole Picador team, for their mastery and spirit

Molly Friedrich, Lucy Carson, Caspian Dennis, and Hannah Brattesani, for their good sense

Mitch Wieland, Brady Udall, Denis Johnson, Emily Ruskovich, Paul Rykken, and Carol Hornby, for resonant guidance

Joy Williams, for her fire

Mary Pauline Lowry, for her generosity

My family, for taking me seriously and making me laugh

and, most of all, Travis, for everything.